Moonlight Ride

Moonlight Ride

Lexi Bassford

Copyright © 2010 by Lexi Bassford.

Library of Congress Control Number: 2009906517
ISBN: Softcover   978-1-4415-5123-8

All rights reserved. No part of this book may be reproduced or transmitted in any form or by any means, electronic or mechanical, including photocopying, recording, or by any information storage and retrieval system, without permission in writing from the copyright owner.

This is a work of fiction. Names, characters, places and incidents either are the product of the author's imagination or are used fictitiously, and any resemblance to any actual persons, living or dead, events, or locales is entirely coincidental.

This book was printed in the United States of America.

To order additional copies of this book, contact:
Xlibris Corporation
1-888-795-4274
www.Xlibris.com
Orders@Xlibris.com
60695

CHAPTER 1

A SMALL VALLEY appeared through the early morning fog. The sun started to climb above the snow-kissed Colorado Mountains, slowly melting the misty fog and sweeping away the darkness and stars. Through the early morning haze, high on a groove in the limestone valley wall was the faint outline of a black figure, guarding the valley as a king.

* * *

A silent hawk sliced through the turquoise sky; melting into the blazing late July sun then reappearing again. A red fox darted from one clump of sagebrush to another and a jackrabbit sprang from shadow to shadow. A bird's song flew ahead of them into the lucid blue sky. Does and their fawns grazed quietly under the shade of the towering pine trees and a soft breeze brushed through the lofty oak trees that stood by the clear brook that surged through the valley. In the stream, little silver and green fish raced. Long grass and purple, yellow, blue and pink wildflowers danced in the wind like a stunning moving watercolor painting.

Hoof beats echoed in the distance as the ground started to tremble. The lone jackrabbit disappeared into his burrow. The deer shied and trotted off with their fawns right behind them, white tails flashing. A multicolored wave of wild horses flew over the green sloping hills that rolled over the valley floor. Then, a tall honey colored mare with a white glossy mane led the band through the open plain to the thin stream that whispered to itself quietly. A tall black stallion came up from behind. Sweat shone on the bulging muscles that pumped under the black hide. His legs scissored back and forth, flashing three white stockings, black hooves hammering the hard ground he flew over. He surged through the band of horses and then took the lead. The stallion threw his head up, sweeping away the long, thick black forelock that hung over his fiery brown eyes. The white star on his forehead shone in the bright sunlight. His hooves pounded the sandy earth around the stream. He snorted and then shook his small, but handsome head. The thick black tail that touched the wet ground beneath him flicked at the yellow striped deer flies that buzzed around his hocks.

The stallion's head fit perfectly onto the long and elegant neck that showed his Arabian conformation with a trace of his Mustang blood. His long mane reached down to his shoulder – though matted with burrs and mud was beautiful. His only visible defect was on his left foreleg; a long scar marred the black skin that ran from his knee and then stopped at his hoof. Mares crowded each other at the edge of the brook and a pregnant mare, just the color of ink with a white appaloosa blanket marking draped across her back lowered herself into the sand and rolled in sheer joy to be a horse. She rolled over and somehow gracefully lifted herself back up. She then shook like a large, wet dog as water droplets and grains of sand flew in all directions.

The black stallion lowered his head and sipped from the cold stream. Suddenly his ears pricked and his head flew up. Then he stood still, perfectly shaped ears listening intently, nostrils flared. Water dripped from his muzzle and splattered on the sandy ground. The stallion wheeled backwards and trotted up to the sheer rock wall of the valley. A wide crack looking like a shadow from a distance split the stone. He vanished into the narrow crack which was just wide enough for a horse to fit through. He reappeared higher up on a ledge where he watched over his band and the honey-colored lead mare watched them from the valley floor.

A small strawberry roan filly waded into the chilly water up to her little chest and sucked up a long drink. She squealed and started blowing on the water with her fuzzy muzzle, splashing up tiny droplets of water that shone in the sunlight. Her mother, a chestnut mare, quietly grazed with the other mares that whickered softly to their foals by the shallow water around the bank. Their petite hooves pressed prints in the soft streambed and then the prints were washed away by the clear water.

The roan filly waded back to shore and started splashing with the colts and fillies as their father kept watch from his ledge.

* * *

Ten miles away, a black truck revved its engine. Duly tires crunched on the gravel driveway as it drove, pulling a silver metal trailer behind it. A whinny could be heard from the inside, accompanied by a kick from a shoed hoof. The big black door of the truck read "Starlight Ranch". The truck rolled down the gravel drive and past a large red barn. Whinnies and nickers floated through the open doors along with blaring country music.

A tall, attractive girl around fifteen years old came walking out of the open fire engine red doors. She was leading a slightly limping palomino gelding out of the barn. The palomino was smallish and shone gold in the sunlight. The girl guided him into a large rectangular corral where another bay gelding was already cantering up and down the long fence. The girl led the horse up to the gate and unlatched it. She reached for the clip on the lead rope and unfastened it from the blue halter. The palomino walked into the corral, whickered, bucked twice, then cantered over to the other gelding and fell right into step with the larger horse, their manes and tails floating in the warm afternoon air.

Caidy McKinney perched on the white fence and blissfully watched her family's beautiful horses galloping in the corral. She could make out more of their horses grazing in the green pastures beyond. She was a tall, slim girl, with long, wavy blond hair pulled back into a pony tail. She let the gaze of her sky blue eyes fall upon the Rocky Mountains. The snowcaps were vivid white, as if God had thrown a white sheet over them.

She trotted over to another corral. As she leaned on the fence, she felt a little nudge on the leg of her faded, ripped blue jeans. This was Kitty's corral. Kitty was a two week-old palomino filly whose mother had probably been a Mustang. Caidy had been riding one night a few nights before and had seen a flash of something shining in the bright moonlight. She had found Kitty, a filly who had somehow been left behind by her herd. If Caidy had been any later, the foal would have remained coyote bait and more than likely would have attracted one. She had carried the starving filly over her horse's shoulders. When she brought the foal back to the ranch, she had given her to a mare named Princess – whose own foal had died. Princess took in the mustang filly, instantly accepting and caring for Kitty as her own.

Kitty's little cream mane was so short that it stood straight up in little tufts like brand new chicken fluff on her little neck and she did not have a forelock at all. Her short, bushy tail waved back and forth like a little flag. Caidy laughed and touched the filly's soft muzzle. Kitty snorted and nibbled at Caidy's short pink polished nails. Princess trotted up to Caidy and whickered and nuzzled her long blond hair. Caidy smiled and massaged the white upside down heart on Princess's forehead. The heart stood out on Princess's blood bay coat that shone from her early morning grooming.

"Well," she whispered to the two horses on the other side of the fence, "I'd better get back to work; see you two later."

She turned around and sauntered back to the giant barn that stood in her own backyard. As she walked through the door, she stopped and took in the sounds and smells of the stable that she loved so much. She heard horses whickering, snorting and crunching hay. She smelled the sweet scent of alfalfa hay, the great aroma of horses, leather, and the bitter perfume of the strong coffee brewing in the barn office. Caidy started walking and almost tripped on Yo-Yo, one of the McKinney's barn cats. Her orange body was striped with yellow and her green eyes saw anything and everything that went on at Starlight Ranch. Her tail was marked with obvious kinks, showing that she had broken her tail more than her share of times. Yo-Yo was stretched out on the cold concrete floor of the barn, her long legs stretched as she yawned widely. Then, she leaped up onto a stall door and looked curiously at Caidy as if to say, "What are you looking at?"

Caidy stopped at the office and saw her mom, Crystal McKinney, typing on the laptop at her desk, drinking a cup of coffee and cradling a phone on her shoulder. Crystal looked up with her hazel eyes as her daughter walked by the door of the family office.

"Hey, Honey, what's up?" she asked.

Crystal McKinney had short, curly blond hair with a white headband holding it down and in control. She was tall and thin, like her daughter, and dressed in jeans and a blue, loose Western style button down shirt.

"Chores," Caidy groaned and pretended to sigh dramatically.

Her mom smiled and then went back to talking on the phone and started typing again. Caidy walked up to Black Magic's stall. The mare was due to foal anytime now. The mare had escaped a few months before and had joined Moonlight's herd and was now carrying Moonlight's foal. Caidy's father, Nate, had promised her the foal of the ebony horse that ruled the largest wild herd in Colorado. The black mare looked lazily over her shoulder at Caidy.

"Hey, girl, let's get you outside a little bit." she said as she took the lead rope off of the hook on the stall door.

She slipped in and gently petted the black horse. Magic blew slowly through her whiskery muzzle as she nuzzled her jeans pocket. Caidy smiled as she pulled out a slightly brown apple half. Magic's ears pricked and she lipped the treat out of Caidy's outstretched hand. Magic chewed loudly as Caidy clipped the lead rope onto her white halter. Caidy was trying to think of the perfect name for Magic's foal. She figured she would have to see it first. She led the raven colored horse through the barn aisle and into the bright afternoon sunlight. They both blinked, adjusting their eyes. Caidy led her to a pasture where other horses already grazed. They were faraway specks of black, white, red, palomino and brown – the size of toy horses. Caidy gave Magic a kiss on her nose and unclasped the lead rope. The black horse slowly trotted to the shade of a tall stand of birch and aspen trees and started lazily grazing.

Caidy's tricolored corgi, Fizzy, happily bounced up to Caidy and sat down, looking up at Caidy with a wide smile on her face. Her sparkling brown eyes were locked on Caidy. Fizzy was a short little dog roughly the shape of a fat bratwurst and her eyes looked like they had way too much eyeliner around them and she had a little black nose. Corgis do not have tails, so she just wagged her little bottom. On her brown head, there was a wide white stripe with a single brown dot right in the middle that the McKinney's called an "angel kiss." Her back was black, her shoulders brown, her tummy white and her skin pink. Caidy leaned down and scratched behind her dog's big, rounded, fox-like ears.

Crystal's dog, Pip, always stalked Fizzy close behind; driving the older corgi almost out of her mind. Pip was short for Pipsqueak and he fit his name perfectly. He was a very small, white fluffy, loveable dog who was always getting himself into trouble. His white fur lay flat in some places, in others, it stuck in all directions. One of Pip's ears stuck straight up, the other flopped halfway down for no apparent reason. He was one half-pint ball of white fur, except for his little button of a nose and loving black eyes that shone through his crazy fur.

Caidy made her way to the tack room at the end of the long barn, disappeared inside, and came back pushing a wheelbarrow with a pitchfork towards one of their stud's stalls and started to muck it out while Fizzy trailed at her heels. This stud was called Golden Fire and he was a palomino – his coat was fiery gold and his mane was white. When she was almost done, she heard a loud, high whinny that meant a hello from Black Magic – a call Caidy had not heard in a long time. Caidy ran out to her horse's corral, stopped and watched her mare, whose big brown eyes watched a gray mountain that rose above a large green pasture.

Caidy made out a stallion's scream that she would have recognized anywhere. It was a scream that gave her goose bumps. There was a small cloud of dust floating over the mountain kicked up by untamed hooves. If anyone had been close enough to hear her, they would have heard Caidy whisper, "Moonlight, you came back."

CHAPTER 2

THE DEEP DARKNESS that covered the night was broken only by the bright pinpoint stars that gave the ranch its name. On the mountainside, the wild horses' heads were down, half asleep but the jet black stallion was wide awake, slowly walking through his herd of mustangs. His black coat glistened in the soft moonlight. His eyes were alert and his long mane gently floated in the nighttime breeze. Crickets were chirping to the sleeping world and an owl shrieked from a distance. Foals were lying asleep in the tall grass under the sky and bats fluttered above, squeaking and chattering quietly to themselves. The mighty mustang stallion, called Moonlight by the ranchers in Colorado, hung his head and fell into a light sleep.

The next day, the sun rose once again over the mountains, this time shining on large billowing thunderheads that loomed over the rugged land. Moonlight was again on his ledge, watching over the grazing mares and his foals buck at the sky that the clouds were wrapping. Lightning flickered in the distance and thunder rumbled angrily. The black clouds continued to slowly creep over the sky, blocking the bright sun. The horses' ears flicked as the rain started to drop on them and then the drops stood like shining diamonds on their glossy hair. The drizzling rain turned to large drops that came down harder and harder, darkening the dusty ground beneath their hooves.

The lightning crackled above them and the thunder growled in the black clouds that now seemed to stand still over the valley. The grass and wildflowers gratefully soaked up the welcoming rain and the thin brook soon started to swell and flow over the boundaries it had known before. The towering oak tree leaves danced in the strong wind that whistled through them. The foals trotted in the ever hardening rain towards their dams that nuzzled them.

Moonlight's black mane stuck to his neck and the rain splattered on his black body as he loped to the huddled group of horses under the pine trees. The rain continued to pelt down from the somber clouds that hovered above the horses.

* * *

The rain pattered on the windshield of the black truck as it rolled across the asphalt that stretched out across the flat plain. The windshield wipers flashed wildly, spitting rainwater.

Caidy switched the radio to the Country station. She sighed contentedly as she watched the rain race down the window. She glanced over and looked at her dad. He was staring straight out the windshield at the black road that kept appearing before them. He had been in the barn all night with a mare who had become the mother of a beautiful colt who was the color of fresh snow.

As the rain slowed, Caidy turned and looked through the rear window at the trailer they were pulling. One of their palomino mares, Desert Storm, was inside. Caidy settled back into her seat and kept her gaze out her passenger window. Across the plain, she saw a slight movement. As she looked closer, she saw a large herd of horses galloping across the smooth ground.

"Hey, Dad. Look," Caidy said in a soft voice, not moving her gaze from the horses. "There they are . . . the wild horses. I haven't seen them in a long time."

"Yeah, I ain't seen 'em much either." Nate replied as he leaned to glance out her window to take a look.

The rain started to come down faster and the horses disappeared as the white rain created a wall between them. A rod iron gate appeared on the side of the road. The main gate was huge and had a forged image of a mare and a foal trotting on it. Their diesel truck slowed down and then stopped. The small camera at the top of the fence revolved and focused on the truck. Then, the gate slowly swung open and the truck rolled up the two-mile long driveway. Through the rain, Caidy could see white fences slowly pass by. Miniature horses stood and grazed quietly in the wet grass. They drove up to an enormous pristine white barn, at least two times the size of the red barn at Starlight ranch. Her dad parked the truck and Caidy hopped out and headed for the trailer as her dad made his way towards Mr. Randall, the owner of Randall Ranch. There was a loud stamp from inside the trailer.

"Hang on, girly," she softly whispered to the horse.

Caidy unlatched the door of the trailer and swung it open. She was getting soaked – her hair was plastered down to her head and her jeans were dripping wet. She edged her way to the front of the trailer to the golden horse's head and unhooked the rope from the ring. The big horse backed out into the rain. She led Desert over to her father and the owner of the ranch, who were standing just inside the barn. Mr. John Randall looked over to her. His enormous white cowboy hat made him look as if he was about to lose his balance and his white and black striped snakeskin boots, with two inch high heels, did not help either.

"Well," he drawled, trying to sound like a real cowboy and failing in the attempt, "if it ain't the pretty little lady," Caidy tried to smile, not knowing if he was talking to her or the horse.

"Hi, Mr. Randall," Caidy answered, just to be safe.

Mr. Randall looked at Caidy in surprise.

"Oh, um, hello," he said and then turned his attention back to the horse she was holding.

Caidy's cheeks heated in an embarrassed blush. So he had been talking to Desert.

Desert shook her head and snorted, uncertain of the stranger.

"Wow, sure is a wild one! Sure hope she won't go loco on me!" Mr. Randall exclaimed.

Caidy had to use all her willpower to keep herself from laughing. What would happen if he ever messed with an actual loco horse? Caidy looked over at her dad and saw that he was looking at the New York City native and was not sure what to think either. Mr. Randall was looking Desert Storm over – like he really knew what he was doing.

"Yep, she looks in perfect shape. I'll write ya the check in just a sec," he said, matter-of-factly. He had made an incredible offer on the mare. They had been trying to find an owner for her and Starlight Ranch sure could use the money. Nate had only accepted John's offer because one of his high school buddies was the head trainer at the Randall Ranch and he had promised to care for and train Desert personally.

Caidy leaned on the large barn door and looked outside. The McKinney family had owned the mare for as long as she could remember and she did not want to lose her to the Randalls.

Nate bought abused and abandoned horses for hardly any money, got them into top shape again, then sold them for thousands more than he had paid for them. Caidy was used to the idea of losing horses, but that did not mean she had to like it.

Through the sheets of rain, Caidy strained to see a sports car driving up to the barn door. The flashy lime green sports car pulled up to the barn doors and stopped. The door opened, Maddison Randall opened a hot pink umbrella and then stepped out. She paraded into the barn, closed her umbrella and hung it on a hook outside a stall. The girl was five foot nothing, but her high-heeled shoes made her about four inches taller. Her shoulder length hair was arranged in perfect coffee brown curls and her nails were manicured and painted bright pink. She was unfair pretty. Her brand-name jeans were too tight and she was wearing a yellow tube top that would have looked like a feed bag on anyone else – somehow, though, on her it did not. Maddison's eyes were heavy with mascara, eyeliner and eye shadow and too much of it at that. Caidy wondered how she could even keep her eyes open.

Maddison brushed right past Caidy as if she was not there and strutted like a peacock right up to Mr. Randall.

"Daddy, I need some money. I'm going to the mall in Denver," she said, sighing disdainfully. Nate stared in amazement at the spoiled teenage girl.

"Okay, honey," John cooed. He reached into his pocket and pulled out a bulging wallet.

He opened it and Caidy barely kept herself from gasping. She had never seen so many hundred dollar bills all at once. John pulled out three and handed them to his daughter. Caidy's eyes widened as the girl snatched them, rolled her eyes and sighed. John gave her two more and then got a tiny, forced smile from his daughter.

"Have fun, honey." Mr. Randall told his daughter.

She gracefully took her umbrella off the hook, made a show of opening it and then flounced out into the rain to the sports car that sat in front of the barn. A ranch hand opened the door for her and she got into the car that might have actually cost more than the McKinney's house. Caidy's dad did not seem surprised at the rich girl's attitude either.

"Where do ya want the horse?" Nate asked gently.

"Over there in that stall." Mr. Randall said as he absently pointed to a stall while he lovingly rearranged the money in his still open wallet.

Caidy started leading Dessert Storm toward her new stall. She led her in and looked in disgust at the stall floor. At their ranch, the stalls had at least three inches of bedding, no matter how much money it took. Here she doubted that there was half an inch. Obviously, the Randalls could afford to spend a few extra dollars on bedding.

As she looked around, she noticed that the water was clean and full and the hay rack was overflowing with fresh golden hay that matched Desert's coat. She unhooked the lead rope and slipped out of the stall.

"Well, little lady," Mr. Randall attempted to sound cowboy again, "Why don't you walk around and look at all the pretty horses?"

Caidy smiled. As Mr. Randall talked about all the details of the sale and her father listened, Caidy wandered around the huge barn. She overheard Mr. Randall say: "You know, no offense to your horse, of course she's a dandy, but there's one horse that I really want that I haven't been able to get. Oh, I've been able to get him, alright; I just haven't been able to keep my hands on him. That loco thing keeps getting away." He followed up with a laugh that bordered cruel. The way he did it gave her goose bumps. Caidy knew exactly which horse he was talking about – Moonlight. She and everyone else in Bailey knew that he'd had him right on this very ranch a couple of times before, but Moonlight had always been able to escape. What if Moonlight was not lucky enough to pull it off the next time? There was also a rumor floating around town that John Randall had been the one who had placed the long, jagged scar on Moonlights foreleg. No one had any proof of that, but it was pretty darn likely.

She heard the men lower their voices. She pushed all those thoughts out of her head by looking at the expensive horses. They were all beautiful, but they looked sick and tired of their stalls. As she walked up to one stall, she noticed the probably real gold name plate attached to the door of the enormous stall. It read: "Dawn Dancer, Maddison's Pride and Joy." Maddison's pride and joy? She had probably only laid eyes on the horse when she took all her snobby friends on a tour to show them how much they had and she probably hardly ever had ridden the gorgeous mare.

Sure, she had hired extremely famous dressage riders from all over the world to train Dawn Dancer for world-class championships. Dancer had done beautifully and had won first place in several shows, but Maddison had done absolutely nothing to help her mare rise to the top. Caidy doubted Maddison really even knew how to ride well. She just jumped on at the show and expected the horse to take it from there.

Caidy looked at Dawn Dancer. She was a beautiful strawberry roan mare, about five years old. Her mane and tail were cream and her hooves were black. She was one of the most beautiful horses Caidy had ever seen. The horse looked at Caidy with big brown soft eyes and whinnied. Nate walked up to the stall door.

"You ready to go?" Caidy asked hopefully.

"Yep," Nate answered.

Walking out to the truck, Caidy was looking around.

"Big place, huh?" she asked.

"Yep," he answered again.

He opened the door for her and she climbed in.

When the truck was rolling on the asphalt road, her father fell into one of his cowboy silences. The rain had stopped, but the dusky clouds still hung over them.

"Caidy?" he suddenly asked.

"Yes, sir?"

"Thanks for not being like Maddison," he said looking straight at her.

She hesitated, a smile threatening to make it to her face. She had not seen that one coming. She smiled happily. A trace of something like a smile crossed Nate's tan face. He had always gotten very shy whenever he gave compliments, because, after all, he was one hundred percent, total, hard core cowboy.

As she gazed out the window at the barren land around her, a strange feeling gripped her. Her spine felt like cold raindrops were rolling down her back and goose bumps skittered across her arms. Even though she looked closely, she could not imagine what was making her feel that way.

As she looked out the windshield again, the truck screeched to a stop as a herd of wild horses streamed across the road in front of the truck.

Moonlight had been watching over his herd on the open plain on which the road snaked through like the stream in his own valley. The smoky stallion had watched the large black truck drive down the road. He watched his herd graze in the scarce grass that was spread around the valley floor. The pine trees around the edges of the valley blew in the wind that whistled through the valley. A downpour started once more.

Moonlight's head flew up, his ears pointed towards the sky. His nostrils flared and he stood motionless, testing the wind while his eyes searched the trees around his herd. The lead mare also smelled the wind as some of the mares in the herd started getting nervous, but did not dare bolt until they received the signal from her. The stallion's muscles twitched under his black coat. He gave an invisible signal to his mare. She gave the signal to the herd and they started galloping towards the road. Moonlight moved towards the herd that was going through the small valley towards the mountains. They quickly approached the road; the mares were blinded by the fear that told them to run. As the large truck screeched to a stop in front of them, they cleared the road and broke into a gait just above a gallop and ran towards the mountains.

As the truck started slowly moving up the road again, Caidy gasped aloud as she looked into the rearview mirror and saw an ebony stallion evaporate into the rain that pounded the valley floor.

She recognized the stallion. It was the black horse that galloped through her dreams every night. It was the father of her future foal. It was the stallion she had loved from first sight.

CHAPTER 3

CAIDY RODE AN untamed black stallion as he galloped across a flat stretch of ground. Her fingers were wrapped around the coarse black mane that flung back and stung her face and arms. Her legs gripped the horse's back as she hung on to the soaring horse.

They were one heart, flying across the ground. His leg pumped as effortlessly as if he had wings. His ears were pinned back against the wind and his tail was flowing behind him. Caidy was clinging to his neck as jet black mane and blond hair blended together. They were running as if they would never stop. They would run until they ran out of ground and heart. Caidy was in pure bliss as she rode the stallion she loved.

BEEP! BEEP! BEEP! Caidy's alarm clock startled her out of her dream. She groaned and squinted at the glowing turquoise numbers on the clock – 4:01. She slapped the snooze button, groaned again, rolled over and crammed a pillow over her head.

Fifteen minutes later, *BEEP! BEEP! BEEP!* This time, she sat up, yawned and stretched. She flipped on her lamp and stepped over a sleeping Fizzy to open one of her drawers. She tugged on the first pair of jeans her fingers touched and a t-shirt. She pulled a brush through her thick hair and brushed her teeth. Making her bed could wait until after breakfast. She bounded down the stairs two at a time with Fizzy trotting after her and started on her chores. She plugged in the coffee maker and dumped coffee grounds and water in, then walked out to the chicken house carrying a large wicker basket. Caidy could already smell bacon cooking in the bunkhouse where the ranch hands lived. She would have to be quick to make up for that extra fifteen minutes of sleep. Caidy walked into the large chicken house and started collecting eggs. Then, she carried the full basket back to the kitchen. She knew that Nate had already gone out to the barn to check on the late pregnant mares. Caidy set the bacon on and started cracking eggs into a large skillet. When one batch was done, she would move them onto a plate and start another one. She did the same with the bacon. She and her mother took turns making breakfast every other week. She also dumped a cup of dog kibble into Fizzy and then Pip's dishes. When she was pouring milk and orange juice into three tall glasses, her mom came down the stairs, also in jeans and a t-shirt.

"Mornin', Mom," Caidy said. Crystal smiled sleepily. She was not a big morning person.

As Caidy handed her a cup of coffee, Nate came in from the barn and sat down at the breakfast table.

"The mares are fine," He said, as usual not wasting much time with words.

They ate their breakfast in comfortable silence and when they were done, Crystal offered to clean up. Caidy ran upstairs to make her bed and then bounded to the kitchen door to the pile of boots that lay there. She dug out hers and pulled them on over her Mickey Mouse socks. Once outside, she tossed chicken scratch to the hens and chicks, stuffed hay nets, refilled water troughs, fed Yo-Yo and measured grain.

She finished just in time to see the sunrise. It first peeked over the tops of the mountains and the sun's rays lit up the early morning sky. The sun rose with red and purple clouds floating around it above the soaring mountains.

She knew somewhere out there, the midnight horse in her dream galloped without her.

* * *

As she ate pizza in the food court at the Mustang Mall in the small town of Bailey, she listened to her best friend, Kimmy talk about a cowgirl hat she had seen the last time she was at the mall and had finally saved enough money for it.

Kimmy had all A's in school. She's the nicest girl in the world and drop-dead gorgeous. Her wavy brown hair with blond and auburn highlights flowed down to her shoulders. She had green eyes, clear skin and perfect teeth. Caidy knew that Maddison Randall was deathly jealous of her, which is pretty darn hard to accomplish. When Kimmy stopped talking to eat her chinese fried rice and egg fou something, Caidy asked her.

"Hey, Kimmy?"

"Hmm?" she answered through a mouthful.

"Did you hear that Moonlight's back?"

After swallowing, Kimmy answered, "Nope, wonder where he was," she drawled, looking closely at her friend.

"You still want him, don't you?" she asked, totally knowing the answer.

Caidy had never been very interested in silly flirting with guys, over-the-top make-up, expensive clothes or many things that most other fifteen years old girls were consumed with. Sure, she thought they were okay, maybe even fun every once in a while, but she did not obsess over them. Her passion had always been horses – Kimmy was the same. The reason both of them came to the mall so much was the Pittsburg Tack Shop (why it was called that, no one knew) and for the fabulous pizza from the food court. The pizza was a dollar for a slice and it was loaded down with every topping imaginable, except anchovies. Caidy could not stand little fish on her pizza. Each slice was about a foot long and just as wide. When they had finished eating they got up and threw away their garbage.

"Hey, look who's coming," Kimmy sighed.

Maddison Randall strutted out of the one and only expensive shop in Bailey and her followers, mostly girls from their school, Bailey High School, were loaded down with bags – probably Maddison's. Caidy was surprised to see her there. She usually shopped in the huge malls in Denver which was about an hour away. Maddison took in their jeans, knit shirts and tennis shoes in one superior look and sneered.

"Well, if it isn't the little cattle girls!" she laughed.

"If you mean cowgirls, you're right on." Caidy said. She heard Kimmy laughing behind her hand, trying to act like she wasn't. Caidy did not even try to hide her own smile.

"Whatever," Maddison snapped.

"Yuck, you smell like horses," Maddison's lead follower, Alice, said as she wrinkled her nose. Caidy knew she did not – she had taken a shower before leaving her house.

"Thank you – and, hey, you smell like, um, let me see, French vanilla cappuccinos?" Caidy said smoothly, swallowing her laughter. She and Kimmy walked away towards the tack shop, still smiling.

"Imbeciles, I bet you don't even know . . ." Maddison snorted after them.

Kimmy rolled her eyes as they walked away; glad the rich girl's voice was fading away. Caidy loved it when that happened. She looked into the shop windows as they walked by. Caidy came to a complete stop when they passed a statue shop. There, standing on a shelf in the glass window of the shop, stood a black horse that stood proudly, mane and tail blowing in an imaginary wind. The horse had three white flashing stockings and brown eyes. It was the exact image of Moonlight. Kimmy followed her gaze and gasped. "That looks exactly like . . ." She did not finish because she was being dragged into the shop by her best friend.

It turned out the horse was $11.98 and Caidy had exactly thirteen dollars in her pocket. The statue was hers. They walked out of the shop and Caidy was carefully carrying the delicate horse inside a bag. Then, they headed to the Pittsburg tack shop. The owner was named Tim Johnson and was the nicest guy, besides her own father of course, on the planet earth. He was engaged to Jennifer Miller, one of Caidy's best friends, even if Jennifer was six years older than she was. At their wedding in

June the next year, Caidy will be her bridesmaid. They walked into the store and Caidy took in the scents that were a huge part of her life. She smelled saddle soap, fresh new leather, rope, alfalfa, apple horse treats, hoof oil and horse feed.

"Hey, girls. How's it going?" Tim asked happily as he saw them come in.

"Great, what's up?" Kimmy asked as she made a beeline for the hat rack. Caidy followed her to it and got the first good look at the hat Kimmy had already taken off the rack. It was a white Stetson with a gold band wrapped around it. Small rhinestones were studded in the band.

"Wow, that is really cool, no wonder you like it so much!" Caidy said eagerly.

Kimmy looked at her watch.

"It's time to meet your mom, let's go."

"Okay." Caidy smiled.

Kimmy paid Tim for the hat and they strolled out of the store.

They met Crystal at the one and only palm tree in Colorado. It was in the middle of the mall and personally, Caidy did not think it was real, though everyone said it was. Her mom was sitting on a bench eating a big pretzel and watching Caidy's little brother, Tyler, sleep in a stroller. He was about four months old and had little peach fuzz hair and azure eyes.

"Hey, you two, you ready to go?"

"Yep," They both answered in unison and then laughed.

"Then let's go."

* * *

Moonlight's herd was quietly grazing in their valley when their king's head flew up and his long ears pricked up. Tamed hoof beats sounded in the distance. His herd fled through a groove between two mountains led by the honey colored mare, vanishing in seconds. Moonlight trotted aggressively towards the ever loudening hoof beats. Two horses appeared with riders. Moonlight wheeled around and cantered and seemed to say: "Oh, come on – is that the best you got?"

He did not know that they did not need to outrun or overpower him. All they needed was to get close. The riders spurred their horses into a gallop after the midnight colored horse. The mustang easily pulled ahead of the expensive trained thoroughbreds.

Moonlight led them into a wooded area, making it harder for the thoroughbreds to maneuver their bulk at their high speed. They followed the stallion back into the open, across a plain of grey slate. As one of the thoroughbreds found another gear he streamed ahead of his partner. His shoed hooves flew up small sparks as they hit the hard ground. He ran faster as his riders spurs found his side and began to dig in and a sharp whip stung his back.

The pursuing horses were breathing heavily and sweat had started to stain their silky bodies. Then one of the cowboys got what he wanted – he got just close enough. A sinister grin marked his tanned face. On his smooth gaited gelding, he pulled out a small gun and aimed. He pulled the trigger. A small dart with a red pouf at the end of it pierced the stallion's pumping muscles. Moonlight felt the small prick and surged ahead even faster, angry now. Suddenly, his vision became blurry. As he stumbled, his left foreleg was gashed by a sharp rock.

The grey thoroughbred gelding slowed and then stopped completely. Its riders cruel smile remained as the mighty horse stumbled and then fell to the ground in a deep sleep.

* * *

When Crystal and her daughter walked into their two-story house after dropping off Kimmy, Crystal said, "Oh, yeah, Hon, Mr. Randall called and said he wanted to talk to you." Caidy froze as she set her precious bag on the kitchen table.

"What did he want?" she asked suspiciously, not remembering when he had ever called the McKinney house.

"He didn't say." Crystal answered, "But he said it was important."

"I'll call him."

As her mother left the kitchen to feed Tyler, she slowly picked up the phone and dialed Mr. Randall's number. As it rang, she prayed it was not what she thought it was. The other end of the line picked up.

"Hello?" a woman's voice answered

"Hi, this is Caidy McKinney and I'm, um, returning Mr. Randall's call."

"Alright, I'll transfer you to Mr. Randall's private suite. Please hold a moment."

"Sure," Caidy said as she rolled her eyes. She jumped as the other line was suddenly alive.

"Hello?" A man's voice asked, obviously forcing a twang.

"Hi, Mr. Randall?" Caidy cautiously answered.

"Ah, hello, Caidy!"

Now she recognized his voice.

"I haven't heard your voice in a month of Mondays," he drawled lazily.

Mr. Randall loved old western sayings. He thought it made him sound like a real cowboy. It didn't. Caidy was pretty sure the saying was a month of Sundays, but she did not say so.

"Um," she started, not sure what to say. "You called?"

"Yep, sure did. I heard you were real good with wild horses. You know, breakin' 'em and stuff."

"I gentle horses, sir." she said carefully. She had that same feeling like cold fingers were skittering down her spine that she always felt when she was forced to talk to this man.

"Of course . . . ." He let his voice trail off, probably not sure what gentling a horse meant.

"I just called to tell you that some of my cowboys brought in a wild one today. A black stallion."

Now Caidy knew for sure. It was Moonlight. The horse she had dreamed about since she had first seen him eight years ago. She felt like she could cry and scream at the people who had somehow been able to trap his free spirit.

"Caidy, you still there?"

Somehow she managed to answer evenly. "Yes, sir."

"So, what I want you to do is come over here and try to calm him down a little. I'd be glad to pay."

"Fine; I'm coming over right now."

She quickly saddled a pinto gelding named Colonel. She swung up onto him and loped to Randall Ranch. As she rode, birds sung cheerfully around her. She ignored them. How could someone do that to a wild animal? Didn't they have any heart? Mr. Randall met her in front of the stables. A stallion's scream pierced her to the heart. She swung off her horse and quickly anchored Colonel to a hitching post as Mr. Randall made his way, teetering, towards her on his high-heeled boots.

"He's been going on like that for a while now," Mr. Randall said, sounding completely unconcerned.

She did everything she could to keep herself from screeching at the man. Only her mother's manner lessons branded on her brain kept her from exploding. She ran over to a small circular corral and stepped up onto the fence. Caidy gasped in horror at what she saw. The proud black mustang king stared in blind panic through the blood and burr matted forelock. His soft mouth was covered with a metal muzzle. A rope halter wrapped around the black head. Another rope was tightly tied to the halter and wrapped countless times around a post the thickness of a telephone pole. The black stallion's chest dripped with crimson blood as he pounded against the post. When it didn't budge, he pulled with all his might against the rope that kept him from running. Blood flowed freely from the wound on his foreleg.

The stallion stood still on shaking legs and gazed towards the mountains that touched the blue sky with their rugged peaks. A brown hawk drifted high above the small round metal pipe corral that held the mustang king captive. The horse's brown eyes closed as a quiet groan escaped the horse. His knees bent and the mustang who had only known freedom fell to the dusty ground, defeated.

Caidy climbed over the high fence and ran over to the horse. She ignored Mr. Randall's warning to get out if he stood back up. She pulled out a small pocketknife and sawed through the thick rope that had held her proud stallion. She felt for a heartbeat. When she heard his heartbeat, loud and strong, she sighed in relief. Caidy unlatched and removed the horrible iron muzzle and halter. The rope had rubbed raw lines into the black face. How could anyone do this to an animal? She threw the halter and muzzle over the fence and moved the bloody forelock away from the closed eyes. A bright white star glowed on the black forehead. She leaned down and whispered into the ear of the horse she loved.

"I love you Moonlight, and I promise to do everything I can to help you."

Caidy climbed over the fence. She was going to talk to Mr. Randall. Not blow up at him, but she was going to get pretty close to it. John Randall came towards her with a smug, proud smile on his face. The look in his eyes said, "Thought I couldn't catch him, didn't you?"

"You do know it's illegal to capture wild horses, right?" Caidy said with fake calm, getting right to the point.

"Well, usually it would be," he drawled, "but in this case, it wasn't."

Caidy's eyes widened questioningly.

"Ya see, that broomtail," Caidy winched at the insult as if it was aimed at her. "and his bunch was grazing on my land." he said, pointing a fat finger at himself as he said it.

"That Sheriff Roy said it would be alright if I rounded up that wild stallion."

Sheriff Roy should not even be sweeping up the courthouse, much less be sheriff. That guys head could be turned with five dollars. He had no control whatsoever over the wild horses. That was the Bureau of Land Management, or the BLM's job. She would call them as soon as she got back home. She was pretty sure that with his injuries, he wouldn't be released; not for a while, anyway.

"He's a beauty, isn't he?" Mr. Randall asked, obviously trying to change the subject.

"Mr. Randall," she repeated, refusing to get distracted and trying not to fly into a rage. "I'd like to buy that horse."

His eyes widened in amazement.

"How much?"

"Three thousand dollars, if the police say's he can't be released, and I'm pretty sure he can't be, at least until that cut heals up. It looks pretty deep to me."

She could see him thinking it over. She knew that he had only wanted to capture Moonlight for bragging rights. Now that he had him, he did not know what to do with him. Sure, he could bring in trainers, but she was standing right in front of him with an offer. Three thousand dollars might not be much for a millionaire, but it would take a wild stallion off his hands.

He said, "I was planning on getting him trained and then giving him to my daughter, but . . ."

Caidy held her breath to keep herself from opening her mouth. She could not picture Moonlight with the cruel bits and spurs the Randall family used.

"But, I guess you can have him."

Caidy swallowed a smile, knowing what came next.

"After, of course, I get the three thousand dollars."

She smiled as she watched him wobble away into his barn, willing him to hurry it up. When she finally could not wait anymore, her cowgirl yell split the afternoon air. She did not care if anyone saw and thought she was as crazy as the horse she had just bought. On the way home, riding Colonel through one of Starlight Ranch's pastures, she planned on a way to break the news to her parents.

For Crystal, it would be fine, but Nate was another story. Caidy had a bank account with all the money, so that was no problem but, for some reason, her father had this thing against mustangs. He was against Black Magic's foal, so how would he feel about a grown, wild stallion? He could be a great stud for Starlight Ranch.

They had plenty of room; she could keep him in the empty pasture. There was also the problem of getting him to Starlight Ranch. When she arrived at the ranch house, she had her main plan figured out. She unsaddled and brushed Colonel and then let him loose in the main pasture. Then a sudden thought struck her. What about Moonlight's herd? A bachelor stallion would probably take over. Was that what she wanted? She did not know yet.

She jogged into the house and looked around. No one was home. They had probably ridden out on the range to check on the cattle. Tyler was probably at the neighboring ranch, being babysat by their grandparents. She started on a fancy supper to butter her parents up. She popped a chocolate cake in the oven, seasoned some chicken and put it on the stove. She made her famous buttermilk biscuits and heated up some vegetables. She also made a large salad. Her family trudged in and looked with pleasure at the dinner on the table, steaming hot with glasses of ice cold milk.

After every crumb of chocolate cake had been eaten, Caidy slowly eased the conversation towards horses. When they were talking about Magic's foal, Caidy started talking about the foals sire. Finally, she just came out and said it.

"Hey, guess what? I bought a horse today with my own money." She acknowledged, just as she had rehearsed it, as if she said it everyday. Her parents froze and stared at her, just as if she did not say it every day.

"You did what?" her mom asked, as if she did not hear right.

"I said, I bought a horse today," Caidy said slowly and then it all came out in a rush of words.

CHAPTER 4

"WOW, I DIDN'T see that one coming," Nate McKinney said as he leaned back in his chair after listening to her explanation.

"I would have done exactly the same thing." Crystal exclaimed.

Nate glanced her way as if to say she was not helping much. He fell into another one of his cowboy silences as he thought. The kitchen clock ticks had never sounded so loud, Caidy thought.

"Here's the deal," he finally said, "You're a good girl. You do your chores all the time. I can't remember when I've had to remind you to do them or had to keep after you to do 'em. You get okay grades," Caidy was not about to argue with that.

"And you do really well with the horses we already have. Plus, you have some kind of gift for taming horses. So," Caidy held her breath. "You can have him."

Caidy squealed and jumped up, hugged her father's neck, then danced around the kitchen. Nate just watched her and smiled and Crystal beamed and touched her husband's hand. Tyler laughed and clapped his chubby little hands just because everyone else was excited. Caidy picked up the phone receiver off the wall and called Kimmy. She answered after the third ring.

"Kimmy, guess what? I bought Moonlight! For only three thousand dollars! And . . ."

"Whoa, girl, slow down, you bought a what, when?"

Caidy laughed and then started over, this time more slowly.

"No way!" Kimmy squealed. "You're kidding me, right! That's so awesome! Just what you wanted! Hang on a second,"

Caidy could hear a very short muffled conversation behind a hand clamped over the phone.

"Uh-huh," Caidy heard a male voice say as Kimmy got back on the phone. Her voice was quieter than it had been before. "Mike said we can all ride over to Mr. Randall's place in his truck to see him,"

Mike was Kimmy's brother. He was a year older and was both of their best friends. His blue Ford truck was old and had pulled horse trailers for who knows how far, but he somehow kept it running smoothly. His real pride and joy was his chocolate brown mare, Durango, who he had raised from a little brown filly.

"He's in pretty bad shape," Caidy said and she told her friend about the gash, bloody chest and broken spirit.

"Which reminds me, I've got to call the BLM. Talk to ya later." Caidy laughed.

"Okay, see you around six tomorrow morning."

Caidy heard a soft click as the other line hung up. She clicked end and dialed. After a few rings, she wondered if anyone would be there this late. She hit herself on her forehead. She should have called earlier. A crisp male voice answered:

"Hello, thank you for calling the Bureau of Land Management. We're sorry, but we can't get to your call right now. Please leave your name, number, and message and we'll get back to you as soon as possible."

She left her message and hung up the phone. Caidy galloped up the stairs and into her room. She lay on her bed and dragged out all of her horse books.

* * *

A black shadow in the night, Moonlight awkwardly trotted around and around his small paddock as he favored his wounded foreleg. His scream floated on the wind as he wanted desperately to run free with the wind whipping through his mane and the fresh mountain air pumping through his lungs.

* * *

Moonlight's lead mare's ears were pricked as a white cloud flew across the valley towards the herd. Silver hooves glided across the ground as white mane billowed against the purple night sky that was studded with stars.

A bachelor stallion strode through the herd that had no stallion, claiming it as his.

* * *

As Caidy closed her books, she piled them under the nightstand next to her bed. She flipped off the floor lamp next to her bed, crawled under her blankets and tried to drift off to sleep. She remembered when she was nine years old. She had watched her father examine a black pregnant mare. The mare's large brown liquid eyes watched every move Caidy made. The mare's belly bulged with a foal that her dad had promised would be Caidy's. That night, the mare probably had been scratching herself or leaning on the gate. She had somehow hit the latch and it flew open. She trotted off and joined the wild herd that roamed free in the mountains. A few day's later, she had given birth to her foal. It had been a black colt with three flashing stockings and brown, fiery eyes like his dams. He had run with his mother's herd until he was a rebellious yearling. Then he had fought the aging stallion who led the then small band. He had won and then become the lead stallion, collecting more mares to add to his herd. Now the wild black stallion king who roamed the rugged trails of the Colorado Rockies would finally be hers. Finally, she dozed off.

Caidy was startled out of her sleep by a large peal of thunder. The rain was hammering on her bedroom window. She rolled over and went back to sleep, dreaming of her stallion.

The next morning, Caidy ran through the early morning mist into their large red barn. She flipped on the overhead light and saw curious horses, heads hanging over their stall doors, looking at Caidy. She loved her life.

After she had saddled her gelding, a grey named Silverado, they galloped out of the barn towards Elliott Ranch to meet Kimmy and Mike. Silverado trotted briskly down a dirt road as Caidy watched the sun rise, she talked to her horse. Silverado was grey with black splotches and a black mane, and tail streaked with grey. His grey ears flicked back to catch her voice. As the mist lifted from the earth, sunlight sifted through the canopy of oak, aspen and birch trees and sunrays lit up streaks of early morning air.

As Elliott Ranch came into view, the Elliott's German shepherd came out to greet her and then trotted alongside the tall grey pinto. Caidy swung out of the large western saddle and tied her horse to the hitching post.

Mike walked out of the barn and sauntered towards her. He was tall, lean and what most girls would call cute. He had long curly brown hair and brown eyes with a hint of hazel. He wore jeans and a blue plaid button-down shirt and his black Stetson. Mike was hard-core cowboy. He always wore his Stetson. If a volcano erupted (which in central Colorado is unlikely) and he had to jump out of bed to run from hot lava to save his life, he would grab his hat first.

Also, to be a real cowboy, you do not talk much at all. Caidy could probably count the sentences she had heard him say her entire life and it was extremely hard to out-silence him. Caidy could remember the one time she had done it. Once.

He nodded at her, brown eyes sparkling and she knew he had something to tell her, but she was going to have to ask. That drove her crazy. Kimmy came running out of the house and stroked Silverado.

"C'mon, let's put Silverado in a stall," she said as Caidy untied him from the hitching post and guided him towards the barn. After she got Silverado settled, she and Kimmy climbed into the blue truck that waited in the driveway. Caidy sat in the middle of the brother and sister. The old truck bumped along the dirt road that was a lot smoother on horseback. Soon they reached the paved driveway that led to Randall Ranch.

She knew Mike could not stand the rich New York family. She had heard him say more than once that they should have stayed there. Everyone knew they fit in better with all the ritzy shops, restaurants and hotels than all the tumbleweeds, horses and snow that were in Colorado. So far, John Randall and his mansion style house on the man-made hill on his ranch were fitting in just as well as a cat in a dog show, misplaced and fair game.

They rode past the miniature horses and the normal sized horses that still grazed in the green pastures. Through the open windows of the truck, she heard a stallion calling out angrily.

Mike parked the truck and they all crawled out and then ran towards the paddock where the proud stallion was kept. Caidy had gotten a hold of the BLM that morning and a tall man in a khaki uniform was already standing outside the paddock. The man turned around when he heard them approaching. He was tall and slightly attractive. He had flashing green eyes and perfectly combed and placed blond hair. He smiled, showing faultless, white teeth. His khaki uniform was flawlessly pressed and his nails were clean and had what looked like a manicure. He did not look like he belonged in a horse corral at all and like he had never cleaned a stall or corral in his life.

"Hello," he smiled, "I am Henry Prescott, BLM deputy." he said as he held out his hand. Caidy shook it, then, so did Kimmy and Mike.

"Yes, that horse is not in very good shape at all, but I cannot do anything against Mr. Randall. He has a written permission slip from Sheriff Roy. Apparently, Mr. Randall claimed that this animal was grazing on his land."

Caidy's shoulders unconsciously slumped. "So Sheriff Roy will get most of the blame because he had absolutely no business writing that permission slip." he said. Caidy brightened up again.

"But can't you charge Mr. Randall for animal abuse? I mean, look at Moonlight's leg." Kimmy asked.

"Maybe." The man said hesitantly.

They all stood, watching the stallion. Moonlight stood in a corner of the corral, staring out to the mountains. Henry whistled to him. The stallion's ears flicked towards him, but Moonlight did not look at them. Even when Henry made a clucking sound, Moonlight remained fascinated by something the humans just could not see. Mr. Randall came tottering over to them on his high-heeled, polished snakeskin boots that looked extremely uncomfortable and stood out against all the other dusty brown leather boots the teenagers wore.

"Hello, y'all! Mr. John Randall" he smiled to Henry.

"Hello," Henry chirped and introduced himself.

"Hi, Mr. Randall." Kimmy said.

"Oh, hello, kids," He muttered, turning up his nose at Mike.

Kimmy's eyes widened in shock and Mike's eyes narrowed in anger at the New Yorker's back that was purposely turned on them as he talked with Henry Prescott. Meanwhile, Caidy had climbed over the fence. As she dropped onto the dusty ground, Moonlight whirred around to face her. She did not want Moonlight to feel cornered, so she stood near the edge of the fence, her arms raised like a "T", staring at the black horse, right into his brown eyes that matched Mike's. He snorted, shook his head and then stomped his good foreleg.

There was nothing between her and the wild black stallion but air. He could charge at any second. Caidy kept her position, ignoring the voices of Kimmy explaining to the two men what the heck she was doing. She stood frozen, her boots glued to the hard clay ground that was covered with a thin layer of dust. She stood watching the stallion, every second feeling like an hour. She slowly lowered her arms to her sides.

The horse stopped and stood still, somehow captured by the intense stare held by the stranger who stood in his corral. Caidy had no idea how long it took. She could have been standing there for hours, maybe five minutes. Step by step, slowly he limped over to the blond girl and she slowly cupped her hands. As a black muzzle touched the girl's hand, the wild stallion king gave Caidy some of his trust.

CHAPTER 5

IT WAS PERFECT. The wild stallion was positioned with his muzzle in Caidy's hand. Caidy was standing completely still, hardly daring to breathe as everyone, amazed, watched in silence. In a single second, the spell was shattered. As the lime green sports car drove by, its driver revved the engine and its tires squealed as it spit up gravel and then sped off, just under the speed of sound. As the stallion flinched and his head flew up, his muzzle slammed Caidy's jaw hard, making her bite her tongue. The stallion awkwardly trotted back to the corner where he had been before, wild as ever. Caidy's tongue bled hard as she vaulted over the fence and glared where the sports car had already disappeared.

"You ok?" Mike asked gently.

"I'm fine," Caidy groaned, chin aching.

The policeman and Mr. Randall stood eyes wide in amazement.

"Well, little lady," John Randall started, then stopped, for once actually not quite sure what to say. He was not a cowboy at all.

"Well, that's the best handling of a wild horse I've ever seen, up until the end there. Maybe you can come and help out at the BLM. I'd pay you pretty well," Henry was about to go on, but then his little silver cell phone rang and he flipped it open.

"I'm serious." he said as he turned around and sauntered towards his white truck, leaving a surprised Caidy staring at his back. Was he crazy? Why in the world would he think that she would want to work at the BLM? The state had set up a small ranch of about twenty acres of land that was bordered with white plastic fences. Wild mustangs that had been rounded up off the range were kept here until someone adopted them. And if they didn't, well – Caidy didn't have time to think about that now. She was mad at everyone. Mad at snobby Maddison for revving up her ridiculous expensive little car and mad at the BLM guy for not doing anything at all; mad at Mr. Randall for capturing Moonlight in the first place. Her chin hurt. A lot.

Caidy swung into the truck with her two friends. Mike handed Caidy a handkerchief soaked in cold water. Caidy gratefully took it and held it against her mouth. Kimmy snapped on the radio. The siblings sat in tense silence and watched Caidy. As Caidy listened to the radio, she sensed their stares. She slowly looked over at Kimmy and saw that she was watching her. Caidy glanced over to Mike, he was, too.

"What are you staring at?" she uncertainly asked them both, trying not to move her jaw, but knowing they could understand her. They both quickly stared ahead and seemed not to hear her question. As Kimmy began to sing along with her killer voice that Caidy would have died for, they started to relax. Mike glanced over at the two girls who were sitting next to him. A few minutes later, he glanced over at them and started to say something. Then he stopped. Caidy and Kimmy looked over at him, waiting for him to speak.

Mike looked over, "I think you should bring him to Starlight Ranch as soon as you can." Then he looked straight ahead at the road again.

"But, Mike," Caidy said, "What about his leg? And even if it wasn't torn wide open, there'd be no way to get him in a trailer, and my dad – "

"Walk him over." he said, sounding as if it would be as easy as walking a kitten the five miles it would take to get there.

"Oh, yeah, right," Caidy scoffed, watching Mike.

"No, seriously, you saw how he trusted you, Caidy," He said,

"Yeah and you saw how he freaked out when that stupid car passed by." Caidy said, very much noticing her aching jaw getting worse. She checked for missing teeth and was glad to find that all were present and accounted for.

"Well, okay." Caidy said, hesitating.

"Then do it." Mike said, ending the conversation.

* * *

As the cream-colored stallion stood on Moonlight's ridge, watching over his newly claimed herd, the sunlight glimmered on his silver hide, displaying the faint outlines of dapples on his shoulder. The lead mare stood watching his every move, still not trusting him completely. The foals nibbled on grass and flowers and chased pink and yellow butterflies, unaware of their new leader. The mares grazed anxiously as their eyes followed the colorless stallion who watched over them.

* * *

Caidy collapsed at the kitchen table and closed her eyes, thinking only of her jaw that she was sure was probably black and blue and really swollen by now.

"What's up?"

Caidy jumped as she opened her eyes and saw her dad standing in the kitchen door. He took off his grey Stetson and hung it on the hook that was by the door, showing his long, curly brown hair. Caidy looked at the moonlight pouring in the window above the sink that shone on the floor. Nate flicked on the kitchen light and the moonlight on the floor vanished.

"Oh, nothin' much." she answered.

"Wow," he exclaimed, looking closer at her, "Where'd you get that bruise?" he asked as he opened the refrigerator.

"Is it that bad?" she asked, touching it and then wincing.

He sat down on the chair next to her and set a slice of chocolate cake and a glass of milk in front of her.

"Yep. Now I'm listening."

After explaining, Caidy trudged up the stairs and into her bedroom. She slid into bed under the down comforter and closed her eyes.

"Oh, God," she prayed, "please let this work out."

* * *

The next day, Caidy slowly eased herself over the white fence and into the corral. The black stallion looked at her through a matted forelock. Mr. Randall had received his three thousand dollars, so he mercifully ordered everyone at his ranch to stay away as she moved Moonlight to her ranch. He had already moved on to his next project, who knew what that was. He was done dealing with this horse since he had achieved his goal of just getting a hold of him. Mike stood in the background, making sure everything went as planned. She stood once again, this time, arms relaxed at her sides as she looked at her horse. She had placed the lead rope and soft leather halter over her shoulder so she could easily reach them.

Moonlight watched her every move as she watched his. He finally lowered his head to the ground, lips moving across the ground, pretending to graze on grass that was not there. Caidy knew this was what he would do with a yearling that would have nerve enough to approach him. Moonlight sneaked a look over his shoulder, then, seeing she was still there, turned around again as if to say: "I know you're there, but why should I care?"

Caidy took a small step towards him. He took a small step backward and raised his head in defiance. She took another step forward, and he did not move. She took another and came within reach of him. She wanted to reach out and touch him with every fiber of her being, but waited. The stallion stood, waiting for her to do whatever she was going to do. She eased the leather halter off her shoulder and showed it to him.

"See this?" she said softly, "It's a halter. It won't hurt you and it'll get you out of this place, with crazy cars and crazier people."

Caidy slowly started to move the halter towards his head. He neighed and his head flew back and he quickly backed away. Caidy sighed as she started all over again. She moved towards him again.

"Come on, buddy," she whispered as she took small steps towards the stallion. He seemed to roll his eyes at her as he backed up a few paces. Caidy stopped and then slowly stared to walk away from him. She could almost hear him thinking it out behind her back. Why was she walking away from him? Didn't she want to catch him? Caidy smiled as she heard slow hoof beats coming towards her. She stopped and gradually turned around to face him. She smiled as she saw him cock his head and look at her with inquisitive eyes. She moved towards him quietly.

The wild horse stood still as she slowly eased the halter over his head and gently buckled it. She took the lead rope and clipped it to the halter. She stood next to Moonlight and moved her hand over the soft black coat. Dead hair and dust came flying off. He needed a good brushing, but that would have to wait. His tense muscles relaxed slightly under her touch. She scratched his shoulder and looked at him in surprise when she heard a satisfactory groan. Moonlight had his neck stretched out, eyes closed. When she stopped, he looked back at her, his Arabian neck was perfectly arched. She laughed and started scratching again. She had found his favorite spot.

Caidy gingerly examined his bloody chest and saw that there were only three cuts around two inches long and not very deep. All the rest of the dried blood would wash off.

She stood up straight by Moonlight's head and started walking slowly around the corral. After a few times around, she stopped at the gate. She unlatched it and slowly swung it open.

The girl and the stallion walked through. They started walking down the paved driveway of Randall Ranch towards their new life.

* * *

As they slowly made their way over the old dirt road, Moonlight mouthed Caidy's green plaid shirt. Caidy heard Mike laugh a few hundred yards behind them.

"How can you be so friendly to me and so vicious to everyone else?" Caidy asked the black horse that docilely walked beside her, watching the squirrels that scampered in the trees as if he had not known such an animal existed. Caidy started to inwardly relax but made sure to stay alert as she looked up at the bits of blue sky that peeked through the canopy of oak trees. A gentle breeze blew past them, carrying the faint scent of autumn.

A deer and her nearly grown fawn watched from their cover in the deep shadow of the forest. They watched the muscular stallion and the athletic girl make their way up the dirt road. Caidy led her horse up a small hill and Starlight Ranch came into view. Moonlight's ears pricked up and he looked longingly at the mountains that soared above the ranch. A few seconds later, she heard what he had heard. Another wild stallion's scream pierced the still August air. She tightened her grip on the lead rope and watched the black horse, prepared to let go if necessary. He stood still, looking at the mountains. If he decided to take off, he would rip her right off her feet. She took a step forward and tugged on the lead rope. He advanced, but did not take his gaze from the wild mountains. They walked under the high wooden sign that read with metal letters: "Starlight Ranch." He finally looked around once again at the ranch. Caidy silently sighed in relief.

The corral where she would keep him was still a mile away, near the house. Caidy had always loved her long driveway. As a chipmunk watched them, his cheeks puffed out with some of its stores of food for the upcoming winter, Caidy watched some of the McKinney's saddle horses trot up to the fence and observe the newcomer. Caidy watched Moonlight to see how he would react to the new horses. A big sorrel mare with a yellow flaxen mane and tail named Dixie crowded the other smaller mares and foals to get a good look at the stallion, who she obviously thought was parading just for her. If a horse could sigh like a teenage girl hanging out at the mall seeing an amazingly cute guy walk by, Dixie did. Caidy laughed and led Moonlight to the gate of his own corral that was next to the large pasture so he could socialize with the other horses and could heal his foreleg at the same time. She let him loose. He walked to the middle of his circular corral, lowered himself to the ground and rolled, just happy to be a horse.

Caidy propped up her elbows on the fence, glancing over as Mike sauntered over and did the same.

"Man, he's a great horse." Mike said in a low voice.

* * *

Nate stood outside the barn, waiting for Caidy to appear over the hill that hid the main pasture and corral where she was supposed to keep the stallion. The tall and lean yet still muscular cowboys blue eyes were following a hawk that soared above. Caidy appeared over the hill as Nate watched her approach. As she got to his side, he swung his arm around her shoulders, careful not to brush her bruised jaw. They walked to the tack room and collected the medical supplies they would need to take care of Moonlight's leg; gauze, ointment, a small bucket of soapy water, a sponge and a roll of bandage tape to hold it until the vet could get out.

As they made their way back to the corral, Caidy saw her horse at the fence, head high, ears pricked, nostrils flared, taking in Nate's scent. Caidy lagged behind and let her father walk ahead to "introduce" himself. He walked up to the horse, which stood surprisingly still as he approached him. Nate stood and stroked Moonlight's velvety muzzle. Caidy did not get it. She had never seen a wild horse let people near him so easily. Moonlight accepted him immediately as one of his herd. Nate gently opened the gate, Caidy walked in behind him. He cross-tied Moonlight and looked at his leg from a distance. As Caidy held Moonlight still, her father slowly lifted up his foreleg. Moonlight stomped down hard. Nate stood and rubbed Moonlights side. He tried again. This time, it worked. Moonlight let Nate pick up his leg, but the horse made sure that Nate had to hold it up. After carefully cleaning Moonlight's wound, Nate wrapped his leg. Caidy decided to try to comb out Moonlights mane with her fingers. Nate watched his daughter as she slowly combed out her horse's mane. She pulled out sharp burrs and threw them onto the ground. When she was finally done with his mane, she moved to his forelock. As she untangled it, she looked deep into his eyes. His eyes looked so much like Mike's. Brown and sparkling like he had a secret he would never tell her. The horse's eyes also glimmered with a look that told her he was just barely tolerating her touch.

"Wow," she thought, "His eyes look so much like Mike's." She gasped as she caught herself again. Why was she thinking about Mike so much lately? Well, she could think about him later. She moved her thoughts back to Moonlight. With a soft yellow sponge, she washed the dirt, blood, and dried sweat that covered his face. She breathed in his earthy horse smell and closed her eyes. Her eyes popped open as Moonlight snorted impatiently.

"Sorry, boy," Caidy apologized. She really needed to pay more attention if she did not want to be trampled.

Just as she was finished and had unclipped the crossties, the wild stallion decided he was done standing still. He shook his head and trotted around the corral. The leg, thick with gauze, should heal in a few weeks. She could finish cleaning him up later, when he was more used to her. She was amazed that he could be this gentle.

Caidy walked out the gate and ran up to the house. Her house was two stories tall with black shingles and shutters on the windows. Large oak trees stood in the front yard along with aspen. She trotted up to the wraparound porch that held rocking chairs and small tables. She walked up to the big black front door and opened it. The large living room stretched to a staircase that went up to the second floor. To the left was the large kitchen and to the right was a big sitting room with a grand piano. Beyond that was the master's bedroom. The phone in the kitchen rang.

"Hello?" Caidy answered.

"Hey, girl, what's up?" a voice Caidy recognized chirped.

"Hey, Kimmy, what's up?"

"I just found out that I have to go visit my Grandma, whom I've never met, for a whole weekend."

Caidy knew Kimmy's family was not the closest knit family ever. Her immediate family was fine, but her distant relatives were different.

"That sounds cool," she said, trying to sound supportive.

"Yeah, right," she sighed and Caidy could hear her tired smile. "So that means you'll have to keep Mikey-boy entertained." Caidy laughed, knowing that Mike hated the nickname his little sister had plastered on him ever since she could talk.

"I will. I'll come over tomorrow and help you pack." Caidy said.

"See ya then," Kimmy said and Caidy hung up.

She ran up the stairs to her room. She heard Tyler fussing in his room and Crystal comforting him, trying to get him to go to sleep. She walked into her room and looked around. The walls were painted pink, but the color only peeked through the horse posters and pictures that hung on the wall. Her full-sized bed was covered with a goose-feather quilt her artsy mother had created. Her pillows had embroidered horse heads and horseshoes that Caidy had made. A white dandelion fluff of a dog flashed across the floor and bounded up onto her bed. Pipsqueak sat on Caidy's bed, panting and staring at Caidy as if to say "What?"

Fizzy followed, not as fast, but just as energetic. She lay down and rolled over on the floor, showing her white furry stomach that Caidy petted. Caidy pet Fizzy behind her ears, stepped over her, walked over to the desk and plopped down. She opened her laptop and started typing up an e-mail to her pen pal Johnna Dhani. Johnna lived in Philadelphia, Pennsylvania. She had lived in Bailey, Colorado, but her family had lost their ranch due to foreclosure and they had moved up to Pennsylvania. When they found out they were going to move, Johnna had given Pip to Caidy to keep because they were moving into an apartment complex. Caidy started typing:

> Hey, Johnna! What's up?
>
> You'll never guess what I just did. Remember Moonlight, that stallion that drove your dad half out of his mind because he and his herd would steal hay from your cattle? Well, right after you moved, Moonlight kind of disappeared from the face of the earth. No one knew where he went.
>
> A few weeks ago, he came back with a much bigger band – he has a lot more mares and foals than before.
>
> Anyway, that crazy Mr. Randall somehow got his greedy hands on him. The only thing I know is that he didn't do it the "old-fashioned" way, with ropes and cowboys; he did it with one of those fancy new gizmos he uses. Boy, you know he can afford it!
>
> Well, Moonlight's leg is cut pretty deep, he nearly pounded himself into pieces in that stupid pipe corral they shoved him into and he collapsed, too.
>
> Then I had a great idea. I bought him for $3,000 and Mr. Randall took it.
>
> So now Moonlight is at our ranch in the small pasture, limping around on his poor gashed leg, but looking just as gorgeous as ever.

Everyone says "Hi!" Pip misses you and say's "Hi" too. He's having a great time chasing around my mom's chickens and digging and chewing up anything and everything in sight. ☺

How's Philly going? Do you have many new friends? Kimmy says "Hey". We both miss you so much! Write back!

Luv ya,
Caidy M. ☺

She hit send and clicked the computer closed. Caidy just sat looking out her window at the beautiful land around her house. Mountains soared and swooped across the afternoon sky that was streaked with white clouds that she thought looked like mares' tails. She decided she would go riding, but she needed a partner. She trotted downstairs and into the ranch yard. Chickens scratched at the ground around their chicken house.

Pip had gotten a hold of a light lead rope and was tearing across the ranch yard, entertaining himself. Caidy saw Kevin riding across the ranch on his horse Dingo. Kevin was one of the three ranch hands that worked and lived on Starlight ranch during the summers.

Dingo was a chocolate brown gelding with a rust-colored mane and tail, and had a wide white blaze down his forehead. Kevin's hair was straight, jet black and grew down to his ears. He was sixteen years old and had the greenest eyes Caidy had ever seen. His white cowboy hat was pulled down now, the shadow covering his eyes. He had told Caidy, after having sworn her to secrecy, that he had been an equine gymnast, a person that does all kinds of tricks and flips on the back of cantering horses. Caidy could not picture him doing that.

Caidy walked out to the pasture and bribed Silverado out of the field and then saddled the pinto gelding after Kevin agreed to go. The brown and silver horse loped down the long dirt road that led towards the mountains. They rode up the path that scaled a grey mountain. Soon, they were on a narrow trail. To the right, Caidy's leg brushed the rock wall and to the left, the ground dropped and rolled along the grey wall.

The trail widened and Caidy drew up to Kevin. She glanced at the young cowboy. His face was deeply tanned and his green eyes flashed across the trail in front of him. His long hair was held back with a brown leather string below his white cowboy hat. As their hardy mountain-bred horses continued to climb up the impossibly steep mountain trail, small mountain birds sang out from the small green scrub bushes that grew along the trail. Kevin moved with his horse as one and his brown horse again took the lead at a walk as the horses got crowded.

The trail started to descend and twisted around the mountain. As they reached a narrow, but long valley, Kevin flashed Caidy a challenging smile and Caidy urged Silverado into a smooth gait just above a gallop. She flew across the ground as silver hooves pounded the ground. She heard Dingo flying right behind her. As he drew up beside her, she saw his rust-colored mane billowing. Silver's mane stung Caidy's face as the screaming wind made tears spring into her eyes. Dingo was neck and neck with her gelding as they came to the edge of the valley. Caidy was laughing as she pulled up her horse and he slowed down to a trot. Kevin smiled and laughed with her.

"Nothing beats that, huh?" he asked, still laughing.

"No way," Caidy answered.

They again trotted up a mountain and reached another valley. As they looked down, Caidy gasped. Moonlight's herd stood grazing, miniaturized by distance.

"Hey, look," Caidy said. Kevin looked over Silverado's shoulder.

The honey colored lead mare Caidy had seen before shone in the August sunlight, but something was different. No black stallion stood king of his herd. Instead, a pale stallion stood on a ledge in the valley wall, watching the human's every move.

CHAPTER 6

AS CAIDY WATCHED the white stallion on the high ledge, he trumpeted a warning and galloped into a dark opening she had not noticed before. He reappeared in a smaller cave at ground level and galloped towards them with all the fierceness of a wild stallion. Hoof beats hammered hard earth as Kevin swung Dingo around, Caidy followed him. They galloped on the red dirt trail and started twisting up the mountain. Wild hooves pulled closer and her own horse's hoofbeats vibrated in Caidy's chest. Caidy did not dare look back, but she knew what she would have seen if she had. She would have seen huge muscles pumping under silver hide, fury flickering in his wild black eyes and white mane billowing back into the wind. The stallion was a horse's length behind Caidy, inching closer and closer. She looked ahead and saw Kevin and Dingo ahead of her and then they vanished onto a sharp turn in the trail.

The white stallion snorted viciously. Then, satisfied he had terrified them enough, the stallion stopped, wheeled around and victoriously trotted back to his herd. She slowed Silverado to a trot and drew up to Kevin, who was already stopped. Both of the horses were breathing heavily.

"Wow. Was that awesome or what?" Caidy asked.

"Yeah, but way too close." Kevin answered, laughing. "If you would have gotten hurt back there, I never would have forgiven myself."

They both slid off their horses to check them after their unexpected run. As she ran her hand down Silverado's leg, she told Kevin, "Don't worry; I can take care of myself." As she walked to the back of her horse, she tripped on a loose rock and barely kept her face from slamming down on the hard ground as she fell.

"Hey, are you okay?" Kevin asked, not sounding very concerned.

"Yeah, I'm fine," she answered as she lifted herself off the hard ground.

"Just making sure, since you can 'Take care of yourself,'" Kevin said teasingly and then held his sides and fell to the ground laughing. Caidy smiled as she mounted and pushed Silverado into a trot, leaving Kevin hurrying to mount his horse to catch up with her.

* * *

Moonlight had lost his calm silence and nervously trotted around his paddock. The wild look had returned into his eyes. Fizzy lay in the thick green grass around the paddock and watched the new horse. She looked like she was smiling as her tongue hung out of her mouth.

Pip was rolling on his back in the barn as Caidy walked in and Yo-Yo was watching him in disgust as she groomed herself. Caidy held the heavy Western saddle, bridle and saddle blanket and walked towards the tack room. She oiled the saddle and bridle until they shone in the soft tack room light. Then she hung them on their hooks and walked back to the paddock where Moonlight was kept. He was still trotting restlessly around. Caidy stood on the fence with Marko, the old ranch hand who had worked for her father long before she was born. The old cowboy had hair that was still jet black, but sprinkled with white and grey. His face was deeply tanned and wrinkled from years of looking into the Colorado sun.

Marko was old and as tough as boot leather. His large black cowboy hat had sat on his head for as long as Caidy could remember. Cowboys have this thing for their hats.

His legs were bowed from hours of sitting in a Western saddle and his boots showed they had worked for endless hours.

"Well, at least his leg's feeling better," Caidy said, watching her horse.

"Yep," Marko said. "He's got a lot of wild in him." He continued, "Did you know that there's been a black stallion roaming this range for generations? This horse's father, grandfather, and great-grandfather."

"Really?" She asked, honestly not knowing that.

"Yep, in my lifetime, there's been three of 'em."

"Wow. That is so cool."

"Yep, I read somewhere that thousands of years ago, people said about Arabian horses, something like, 'good horses are pure, clean black, with three leg markings and the right foreleg free: for he is the most precious of the horses'. Yep, you got yourself there one good piece of horse."

* * *

Caidy jogged into the house and saw her mom feeding Tyler out of a baby food jar of squished peas. Caidy recoiled and opened the refrigerator. When she ran out of the house, her jean pockets were bulging with carrots and apples. She trotted to the broodmare barn and stopped at the first stall. Black Magic stood in fluffy hay and waddled over to the door of her stall. All the other broodmares had already foaled and the pastures were full of skinny, awkward, fuzzy foals. Black Magic was very overdue and was going to foal anytime.

Magic joyfully nuzzled Caidy's bulging pockets in anticipation. Caidy laughed and pulled out a bright orange carrot. She broke it into three pieces and held one out on her hand. A gentle black muzzle reached out and lipped up the carrot. Caidy laughed as Magic's whiskers tickled her hand. Caidy popped a small piece of carrot into her own mouth. When they had finished the carrot, Caidy pulled out a brown apple half. Magic squealed happily as she recognized her favorite treat and quickly snatched it up. She chewed blissfully, juice flying from her lips.

"Only the best for my pretty little girl," Caidy said to her horse as she rubbed between her ears.

"Tonight I'm staying with you. Dad will stay with you tomorrow night, then mom after that. You're going to have your baby pretty soon."

Magic whickered, then sauntered off to her water bucket and took several long, slow drinks. Caidy grabbed a bridle on the way to the large pasture that was closest to the ranch house. She opened the gate and walked in, holding a bucket of grain. She shook it, and at the sound, a dozen of the nearest horses lifted their heads and loped towards them. Dixie won as usual. The big sorrel mare thrust her muzzle into the bucket, eating so fast that anyone watching would think she had never eaten before in her life.

"Okay, girl," Caidy said, pushing her brownish head away. All the other horses had flocked around them and were reaching for the grain. Caidy grabbed on Dixie's blue halter and threw the rest of the grain on the grass. The other horses rushed and daintily picked up the pieces of grain from in between the pieces of grass. Dixie glared at Caidy, and if a horse could say "Not fair," she would have.

"C'mon, silly girl," Caidy said as she slipped the Western bridle over her halter. As she buckled it, the other horses, sure they had gotten every piece of grain, galloped off, running with the wind. Caidy led Dixie out the gate and jumped on her bareback. Dixie's head flew up and she galloped out of the ranch gates, glad to be out of the pasture. They dashed over the dirt road; Dixie's head held high as she flew past the gallop into the pace that only could be brought out by a true horseman. Caidy sat up, gripping onto the sorrel with her legs, but not squeezing Dixie. Her fingers wrapped in the flaxen mane, the reins dangling unused. Caidy smiled the smile that is impossible to hold back when you are on a horse that is soaring above the ground. It's a feeling like no other feeling on earth.

They came to a fork in the path. She eased her still galloping horse to the left, the one that led to Elliott Ranch. The other path led to Randall Ranch. As they neared Elliott Ranch, Caidy slowed a reluctant Dixie to a canter, then a trot. She slowed and slid off the big sorrel and tied her to the hitching post. She walked up to the Elliott's house. It was a huge version of a log cabin that should have looked ridiculous, but somehow it did not. It was two stories and had a high, peaked roof and lots of windows.

She walked up the stone steps and onto the porch. There was a potted jasmine by the door. She rang the doorbell and waited. Felicia Elliott answered. Felicia was Kimmy's mom and was just like another mother to Caidy.

Felicia had long brown hair highlighted with natural blond streaks and had hazel eyes.

"Hey, Caidy! I'm glad you came over, Kimmy is leaving tomorrow. She's up in her room, packing. You can go on up."

She saw the family hat shelf that every true cowboy family had by their front door. She saw Felicia's brown cowgirl hat, Kimmy's white one and Mike's Stetson.

Mike and Kimmy's dad, Rick Elliott, had died almost three years before. He had fallen off a galloping horse. He had been hurt so bad he had died the next day at the Denver hospital. Felicia had never really gotten over it.

As Caidy made her way through the living room, she glanced again at the pictures she had looked at so many times before. There were pictures of Caidy, Kimmy and Mike, Felicia and Rick Elliott, and lots and lots of horses. She took the stairs two at a time, turned on the landing and almost ran into Mike.

"Oh, hoy," Caidy said as she slid to a stop.

Her blue eyes took him in with one glance. He had pulled on his dusty brown boots and wore clean blue jeans and a black t-shirt. His brown eyes glittered as usual.

"You going riding?" she asked.

"Yep, we all are." He smiled and then walked past her and continued swiftly down the stairs.

She continued up the stairs and walked into Kimmy's room. The usually tidy room was a mess. Open drawers spilled over with clothes and suitcases were spread out on the unmade bed. Caidy's eyes landed on the long shelf that stretched out above the bed. It was loaded down with trophies Kimmy had won at local rodeos. Caidy had a shelf just like it at her house. They were both barrel racers. That was what she was going to train Magic's foal to do. Kimmy came out of her closet with an armful of clothes and made her way over to the bed.

"Wow, I didn't know I needed so many things just for three days!" she said, pretending to pant under the weight.

"Oh, I know, it really adds up, doesn't it?" Caidy answered, laughing.

"Help me fold this stuff, will you?"

As they folded, Kimmy talked.

"You know what, I think my grandma should have called a little bit ahead to give us a tiny bit of warning before she wanted her 'only precious little granddaughter to come visit her grandmother' two days from then. I've never even met my grandma. She just sends me a present for my birthday every year. You know what, judging by the last present, she still thinks I'm six years old."

Caidy laughed as she remembered what she had received. A whole big box full of little pink fluffy hair ties, a couple of huge, flashy plastic rings shaped like a heart and a pony head, and the worst, a glittery fairy wand with a huge star and pink fluff at the end. Caidy had laughed so hard the first time she had seen them a few months ago, and she knew that Kimmy was the only person on planet earth she would show it to, besides her family. She would not have showed it to Mike either, but she had opened it in front of him. Bless her grandmother's heart, she still saw Kimmy as a five year old little princess.

Caidy had the most incredible grandparents in the world. They were on her father's side and lived on the ranch next to hers. They babysat Tyler all the time and had used to babysit Caidy. When all the clothes were folded, Kimmy sighed.

"Well, I'm stopping now. Let's go for a ride. Mike said he was going to saddle Durango and Jazzy."

Jazzy was Kimmy's mare. Jazzy was short for Jasmine. Jazzy was a black mare with an appaloosa blanket marking draped across her rump and a tiny star on her muzzle. Her mane and tail was black striped with white that stood out incredibly on the sleek black coat.

As they walked out of the house, they saw Dixie and Jazzy tied to the hitching post, Jazzy was bareback as well. The girls untied their horses and hopped on. Kimmy reined Jazzy towards the barn where Mike was riding towards them on Durango. Dixie danced in place, eager to get going. Durango was a full sister to Dixie.

They swung their horses towards the road. The road slanted down into another valley. They all moved their horses into a lope. Black, flaxen and rust-colored tails flew out together. Sorrel, black and brown heads bobbed in unison as forelocks flew back, revealing hidden markings and cowboy hats flew back and were held only by the stampede strings. Tears sprung into Caidy's eyes as the wind screamed around her. She looked down and saw the dusty ground blur by in a streak of brown and green and red.

Caidy wrapped her fingers around mane and reins, feeling the wiry hares and the warm leather. She glanced to her side and saw the black and white blur of Jazzy and Kimmy flying alongside her. The three horses turned at the valley wall and galloped the opposite direction towards Coyote Creek. They galloped past the entrance of Starlight Ranch and slowed to a canter as they reached another trail leading up Cougar Mountain. Mike took the lead, Caidy took the middle and Kimmy brought up the rear.

They could all hear the whisper of Coyote Creek long before they could see it. They rode a turn on the trail, and then, it appeared. Coyote creek was a crystal clear blue creek. Huge birch, aspen and weeping willow trees hung over the water and tall cattails grew on the wild side. A large boulder sat half on the shore, half in the water. They slid off their horses and tied them to a large aspen tree. The horses, despite their run, had hardly broken a sweat. The teenagers walked out to the boulder and sat down. Kimmy lay on her back and stared at the pieces of blue sky that peeked through the thick oak leaves.

"I'm gonna miss you guys so much," Kimmy sighed. "Grandma lives in Denver. I'm gonna hate it."

"C'mon, it won't be that bad. You've been there before, so you know that it's actually pretty cool." Caidy said.

"Well, if you say so, I'll try to have some fun." Kimmy gave in. "But I'll miss you two and the horses and everything." They listened to the Colorado blue birds singing from their hidden places and watched little silver and green fish struggling against the current.

"Well," Mike said, interrupting the silence that had fallen over the woods. "I guess we'd better get going." But he didn't move a muscle, so neither did the two girls.

"C'mon, let's go." he said, finally dragging himself up. He stood over the two girls and looked down on them.

"I said, c'mon, lets go," he said, holding out his hands. Kimmy grabbed one and Caidy grabbed the other. Mike easily pulled them up and started walking to his horse. He swung up on Durango as Caidy and Kimmy untied their horses. Caidy swung onto Dixie and Kimmy onto Jazzy.

Caidy eased into the lead, Kimmy following and Mike brought up the rear. The sun was sinking low in the sky and Caidy still had a long night ahead of her with Magic.

As they reached the large sign that marked the entrance to Starlight Ranch, she eased Dixie towards it. As she said her good-byes and her promise to come over early the next morning to say good-bye to Kimmy, she rode a walking Dixie over the darkening red dirt road.

As she reached Dixie's pasture, she let her horse loose and carried the bridle up to the barn. The overhead lights were turned on and she hung up the bridle in the tack room.

Caidy trotted through the kitchen and up the stairs to her room. She grabbed a sleeping bag, a big pillow and a book for the long night. In the kitchen, she grabbed apples and carrots. She could hear Crystal upstairs with Tyler and she knew that her father was out riding the ranch.

Caidy walked back to the barn, dragging her load with her. She laid out her sleeping bag on the small cot in the stall next to Black Magic's. She walked towards the stall door and fed the midnight black horse a carrot. As Magic chewed contentedly, Caidy made sure the first aid kit was complete, saw the big, white, secondhand bath towels next to her cot and filled Magic's hay net with fresh, golden hay.

Magic's stall had been cleaned spotless earlier that afternoon by the ranch hands. Caidy topped off her water trough and settled down on her cot and started to read a fashion magazine, waiting for Magic's foal to arrive. The last rays of sunlight were streaming through the high barn windows, showing dancing dust floating in the air.

Pigeons, for once, motionless and silent, sat on the rafters and looked down on the pregnant mare as if holding their breaths while they waited for her foal.

Caidy tried to keep her mind on her reading, but it kept wandering to the horse in the stall next to her. She finally had an excuse to jump up from the cot when her mother came walking through the dark night carrying a heavy tray weighed down with Caidy's supper.

As Crystal set the tray on a small table by the cot and pulled the red checkered napkin off of it, Caidy smiled. A large crisp green salad with cubes of cheddar cheese and ranch dressing waited in a glass bowl and several slices of pot roast were steaming on a plate. A large glass of ice cold milk sat with a plate of white rolls, spread thick with fresh golden honey and yellow butter. Caidys stomach growled in anticipation.

"Well, one thing's for sure, I won't starve to death out here," Caidy teased her mother who always cooked way too much, but somehow, they always managed to eat it all.

"That's the whole idea," Crystal answered, smiling. "Here you go," she said, handing her an unopened box of granola bars.

"Now remember, you've got your phone, so if and when the foal is born, you call up to the house for your dad and me. This time, it's all yours, but call if you need us."

"Okay," Caidy answered, patting the small silver cell phone that was in her pocket.

As she watched her mother disappear into the unusually dark night, she felt a mixture of excitement and terror bubbling up inside of her.

She had seen a few foals born before, but this one would be different. Her father had been there before, watching her and making sure she did everything perfectly and to help if anything went wrong. Now she would be all alone. Sure, her parents would be in the house, but it would take them at least five minutes to get to the barn. What could go wrong in that time? She did not want to know, but, she thought there was no guarantee that the foal would even be born tonight. It was weird, she thought, when your parents do not trust you to do something, you feel like they're treating you like a little baby and when they do trust you, you feel terrified you are going to mess everything up – but you would never admit it in a million years.

After checking on Magic, she settled once again on her cot and started eating the feast set out before her and waited.

CHAPTER 7

As the night dragged on, Yo-Yo curled up on a high shelf in the tack room on top of a pile of warm saddle blankets. Fizzy was dozing on the barn floor and Pip had fallen asleep in the comfort of the ranch house.

As Caidy sat on a tack box in the stable hall reading, Magic quietly nibbled on her hay, ears loped to the sides, and her eyes closed in complete relaxation. She would not be foaling anytime soon. Caidys eyes found the small round wall clock by the tack room - 11:19. She had only been out there for about three hours. This waiting was killing her and the whole night was still ahead of her. As a coyote howled in the distance, Caidy shivered and Fizzy's head flew up, ears alert and a deep growl rumbled in her throat.

"It's okay, girly." Caidy assured her dog. At Caidy's voice, Fizzy's head dropped and she fell asleep instantly.

Magic made a shuffling noise in her stall and Caidy jumped up and looked into her stall. Magic looked over her shoulder and the look on her face said "Hey, take it easy." Caidy smiled, sighed and sunk down on the tack box again.

She walked out into the dark night and looked up. Pinpoint stars stuck the black night sky and a sliver of glowing moon hung. She gasped as she saw a shooting star that sprinkled stardust onto the earth. A neigh rung in the crisp night air, drawing Caidy back into the barn like she was on the end of a string. She walked up to the stall and looked in. Magic was looking at her stomach nervously. Caidy gasped. It was time. Magic started walking tight circles around her stall. Caidy glanced at the clock. She had been outside for fifteen minutes.

Then Magic laid down then lifted herself up again, stomach bulging with the foal Caidy would soon see. She groaned, laid down and stayed down as Caidy watched in amazement. Magic breathed heavily and closed her eyes. Suddenly, she stood up again and walked around in tight circles, then laid down again. About fifteen minutes later, Magic's black head raised and looked in the hay next to her. Caidy did the same and gasped.

A tiny, black, shiny filly lay in the hay, breathing for her first time. Magic heaved up onto her feet and looked in joy at the foal she had just become a mother to. The filly's eyes fluttered open and showed Caidy her hazel eyes that barely showed through her thick, long grey eyelashes.

Caidy dialed the house number on her cell phone, but nothing happened. The reception wasn't working, again. It does that a lot if you live out in the middle of nowhere. Caidy slowly opened the stall door and stepped towards the black filly. Magic had moved to her trough and was taking long, deep drinks. Her ears flicked towards Caidy, but the mare did not move. Caidy used the fluffy towels to wipe off the newborn foal. As she cleared the tiny nostrils and rubbed the fluffy black coat, she looked deep into the beautiful hazel eyes that looked up at her. The filly had a group of white markings on her tiny little rump that looked like the stardust that had fallen from the sky had landed on her.

As she quietly clicked the stall door shut, the foal struggled to get up on her long, thin, gangly legs. Magic moved over to her and the filly fell to the stall floor. Magic whickered encouragement to her new filly. The filly tried again and finally rose onto shaking legs. She raised her tiny little head to nurse.

"Oh, yeah," Caidy reminded herself as she fished her cell phone out of her pocket. She dialed the phone of the ranch house.

"Hello?" A drowsy voice answered. Caidy glanced at the clock again. 2:42.

"Mom?" Caidy asked.

"Oh, hey, honey," Crystal said, her voice instantly waking up. "Is it here yet?"

"Yeah, mom, it was about fifteen minutes ago,"

"What is it, a colt or a filly? What color?" Crystal asked, sounding as excited as if it had been her own granddaughter.

"It's a filly, and she's black and-"

"Wait, I'll be right down with Nate, okay?" She quickly hung up the phone and Caidy did the same. She laid on the cot and tried to think of a name for the filly. She was black, she had stardust on her rump, and she was a filly . . .

*   *   *

Caidy slowly opened her eyes. She looked around, trying to place her surroundings. As she stared at the ceiling, she heard a young foal's high whinny. She bolted up as she remembered where she was. She was in the barn and Magic's foal had been born the night before. She must have fallen asleep before her parents had made it to the barn.

Sunlight was flowing into the stall window and songbirds were singing to the early morning air. She looked over the stall door and saw her midnight colored filly lying in the golden hay. Caidy smiled and the filly struggled onto her tiny black hooves and started to nurse again. She filled Magic's hay net and emptied and refilled her water trough with fresh water. When the filly was finished nursing, she fell asleep in the golden hay. As Caidy watched her baby horse, she was dreaming of when she could train her to barrel race. She was so caught up in her dreams that she did not hear someone approaching.

"Hey," a male voice said, startling her out of her day dreams. She wheeled around and saw Mike standing behind her, looking innocently at the foal lying in the stall, a smile playing at the edges of his mouth. She hated when he sneaked up on her like that. He knew she did not like it, so he did it. Caidy rolled her eyes then fixed them on the filly.

"What're you gonna name her?" he asked.

"Don't know yet. What do you think?" she said, asking him the question she knew he wanted her to ask.

"I don't know," he answered and Caidy sighed. She would never get why guys act the way they do, especially this guy.

"Well, I gotta go," he said, starting to walk off.

"Hey, what did you come over for?" she asked.

"Oh, yeah, you wanna go get some breakfast with me and Kimmy?"

"Well, I don't know – I don't want to leave the filly." Caidy started.

"Your mom said to go. She said she'll watch her." he said, giving her no choice.

She knew they were going to go to the only real place to get breakfast in Bailey.

Joni's Diner was the best place in Bailey for greasy food and small town news and lots of it. As the two friends walked out into the early morning air, Caidy shoved her thumbs into her jean pockets and looked down at herself. Her faded blue jeans were soiled, had a fresh rip, and were wet from refilling Magic's water. Her shirt was dirty and wrinkled from sleeping on a cot all night and her blond hair probably had hay in it.

"Let me go get cleaned up," she said, heading towards the house.

"I'm gonna go pick up Kimmy and then we'll come back for you." Mike said, starting up his truck.

After she had taken a quick shower, she slipped into a pair of clean new jeans and a pink button down shirt. She cleaned her boots and pulled them on. She brushed her hair and pulled it back into a relaxed ponytail after she had applied a little makeup. When she stepped out onto the porch, Mike's blue truck was waiting in front of the house. When she had gotten in and slammed the door, Mike took off in his old truck that went surprisingly fast and bumped along the road that was loaded down with potholes. Mike was definitely not the safest driver in the state of Colorado. As she, Mike and Kimmy bumped along the road, Caidy tried to look at the scenery flashing by the windows. She finally gave up and thought. Today she would start halter training Moonlight. Now she would have two horses to train. *Stardust*! The name hit her like a ton of bricks. Stardust would be what she would name the filly. She snapped back to the present when Mike pulled up to the diner.

They all piled out of the truck and walked into the diner. Caidy looked around. It was an old diner. There were several large Coke signs and everything was red or black and white checkered. They slid into one of the cushy red booths. A young waitress named Linda walked up to them with a tray with three glasses of iced water.

Linda was eighteen years old and had been born in Hawaii. She had moved to Colorado with her parents when she was fifteen. She lived with her dad now in the only apartment building in Bailey. Linda's mom had died the year before. She had caramel colored skin and almond shaped brown eyes and thick black hair.

"Hey, what can I get for you guys?" she asked with her silky voice.

"You go first." Mike told Kimmy.

"Okay, I'll have three eggs, fried, two biscuits, two sausage links, and a couple slices of bacon and apple juice please. Thanks!"

Linda had been writing it all down on her pad.

"Got it. Next?" she asked, looking at Caidy.

"Same as Kimmy, but with orange juice please. Thank you." Caidy said.

After Mike had ordered, Linda said, "Hey, Kimmy I heard you're going to Denver. When are you leaving?"

Caidy smiled. It was just like a diner waitress to know everything.

"Right after this, actually." Kimmy answered.

"Okay, have fun! I'll get you your food now."

* * *

After she had said her goodbyes to Kimmy and Mike, they dropped her off at her house. She checked on Moonlight's filly and officially named her "Stardust".

Now she sat on the fence and watched Moonlight. Caidy had torn up a felt blanket and twisted it into a halter. She had it in her hand as she slowly lowered herself into the corral. She stood until he came over to her. She let him sniff the blue felt halter. She looked deep into his eyes and saw tolerating relaxation. She started to slowly slip the halter onto his head. A mischievous look darted into his brown eyes and he wheeled around and trotted to the other side of his corral.

She laughed and chased after him teasingly as she realized all he wanted to do was to play. He squealed and trotted off to the other side of the corral. After fifteen minutes of chasing, she sat down, leaned on a fence post and closed her eyes, breathing heavily. She slightly smiled as she felt hot horse breathe on her face. She hardly dared to breathe as the black stallion touched his muzzle to her hair. She barley opened her eyes, just enough to see his wide black chest right in front of her. His head was lowered and he looked at her right in the face. A questioning stare shone in his eyes. He looked so funny with his head cocked looking at her that she just had to laugh.

He backed away as she stood up. She stroked his ears and she slipped the halter onto his black head. She held onto the piece of blanket that hung from the felt halter and led him around the corral. After around five minutes of leading and following, she slipped the halter off his head. It was almost like he had done this before.

"Good job, boy," she said as she vaulted over the fence.

She walked into the barn past Magic's stall. She saw Stardust nursing and Magic looking bored. She would have to ask her dad if she could let them out into the paddock. Caidy sat on the tack box in the hall and thought of the stallion who now ruled Moonlight's herd. She was glad they would be protected, but she knew which stallion should be guarding the herd.

Moonlight had been settling nicely into his new home and seemed to be losing some of the wild in him. Just then, a stallion's scream reached her ears. She smiled. He was going to prove her wrong. A little squeal from Stardust answered her fathers call. Caidy got goose bumps. He knew his baby was in this barn. How would he have known? He could not see into the barn, but he still somehow knew.

CHAPTER 8

A WEEK LATER, Caidy placed three bunches of bananas in the shopping cart. She was in town, grocery shopping with her mother for the ranch. They had to shop double, for them and the three ranch hands that actually lived on the ranch. As her mom placed a few pounds of apples into the cart, she checked them off of her list. As they piled up all kinds of fruit and vegetables, they talked about the new filly.

"She is the sweetest little foal I've ever seen!" Crystal said.

"Yeah, I know. You know what's so cool?" Caidy said, "Just before she was born, I saw a shooting star fall and it sprinkled stardust all over. That's why I named her that." Caidy said as she heaved a huge bag of rice off a shelf.

"Yep," Crystal replied as she pulled bags of tortillas off another shelf.

"I heard that Mike asked you out to breakfast this morning." Crystal teased as she put gallons of milk into the cart.

"Mom!" Caidy yelped, making a young lady with four children piled into a shopping cart look at her like she was insane.

"What did you mean by that?" she asked, lowering her voice. "Are you crazy?" She asked, now pulling cartons of orange juice.

"Oh, nothing, Caidy," Crystal smiled. "Could you go get another cart honey?" She asked innocently.

Caidy walked to the cart rack and pulled one out. What in the world did she mean by that? She rejoined her mother and helped her carefully put tons of baby food jars and soft baby crackers into the cart. Caidy made a face as she looked at the labels – squished peas, squash, pears, blueberries and spinach. Yuck.

"No, mom seriously, what did you mean by that?" Caidy asked.

"Oh, nothing, Hon. It's just your father and I have been noticing he's been hanging around an awful lot." she grinned.

"Mom, we're best friends and that's it" she answered.

"Yeah, uh-huh." Crystal teased.

"Mom," Caidy sighed.

She started loading all the stuff onto the checkout counter as her cheeks heated in an embarrassed blush.

When they had returned home, Caidy led Moonlight around his corral and talked to him and shared secrets she would never tell anyone else, not even Kimmy.

"Hey, Moonlight. I did notice Mike's been hanging around a lot, but I don't like him like a boyfriend at all – never. I don't think, no, I know he doesn't like me like that either. So why do Mom and Dad think so?"

Moonlight listened soundlessly while she was talking and nodded his head when she was finished as if he understood her.

"See, you don't think so either, do ya, boy?" She asked as she scratched his black ears. He whickered as she tied the felt lead rope to the fence and carefully unwrapped the thick bandage around his leg.

"Wow, boy," she said examining it. "It's healing up really fast. We should be able to go riding before too long," she exclaimed excitedly.

She rewrapped his hoof and patted his wide chest. He nodded his head and snorted as she eased the halter off his head. He walked to the middle of the corral, lowered himself to the dusty ground and rolled, his legs kicking at the hot August air.

* * *

Caidy opened the stall door in excitement.

Today was going to be the day Stardust was going to see her world for the first time. She clipped a lead rope onto Magic's halter and opened the stall door and led Magic out. Stardust stuck to her mother's side like Velcro. As they walked into the ranch yard, Stardust blinked, adjusting her eyes in the bright sunlight. Caidy stopped Magic and Stardust stopped with her.

The filly's eyes opened wide in amazement as she took in her surroundings. She watched the white blur of Pip dashing around the ranch yard with the usual lead rope trailing behind him, the mountains that were scraping the sky and Yo-Yo, who was watching her every move.

Caidy led the two horses into their own paddock that bordered the large pasture. She opened the gate and led them in. She unclipped Magic's lead rope and let her go. She trotted around the paddock, Stardust following like a shadow. Soon, Magic slowed, stopped and then started to graze contentedly. Stardust looked around, sighed happily and sunk down in the long grass to take a nap.

Caidy hurried inside to the smell of dinner. She floated into the dining room and looked at the feast spread out on the table. Fresh burritos bubbled with ground hamburger, melted cheddar cheese, salsa, and sour cream. Fresh golden tortilla chips were piled in a large bowl and an enormous salad sat in a porcelain bowl with fresh lettuce, cucumbers, carrots, tomatoes and onions and dotted with cubes of sharp cheddar cheese.

She sat down with her family and the ranch hands and started eating the fabulous meal her mother had made. The spicy food, cooled down with the salad, tasted amazing.

She looked around at her family and friends. Marko, Nate and Kevin were eating like they never had eaten before. Tyler was eating squished something that Crystal was feeding him. As Crystal poured coffee and scooped mocha caramel ice cream after the dinner dishes had been cleared away, they talked about the horses. Kevin was talking about Magic.

"Yeah, I know, she was really late this year," Nate said as he finished off his ice cream.

Caidy half listened through the swinging kitchen door. She was up to her elbows in soap suds as she washed the dishes and cleaned the kitchen as she looked out the window into the dark night.

She had put Magic and Stardust back in their stall earlier that evening. As she gazed out the kitchen window, she saw a slight movement in the ranch yard. As she tried to look closer, she could not see anything past her own reflection in the window. Then, she could not see any more movement.

She again looked down at the dishes and put her hands into the warm sudsy water. As she distractedly moved to sponge over a plate, she stared out into the night again. The movement was happening again, this time closer to the chicken house. Whatever it was out there was going for the chickens.

She quickly dried her hands and poked her head through the swinging door to the dining room.

"Hey, Daddy, can you come here a minute?" she asked.

Nate got up from the table and walked into the kitchen with Caidy.

"Dad, look out there," she told him, motioning towards the window. "Tell me if you see anything moving."

After he had looked deep into the inky night he said, "Yeah, there's something moving out there, heading to the chicken coop. Let's go check it out. Are you coming?" he asked.

"Yeah," Caidy exclaimed as she walked out the kitchen door with her father, excited to be going with him. As they approached, the movement stopped about three feet from the chicken house.

"He's back," Nate said under his breath.

As Caidy's eyes adjusted to the dark, she saw a dark red animal crouched down in the vegetable garden, trying to be invisible. The fox's pointed muzzle was lying on the dirt and his large ears were pinned down to his reddish-brown head. His long bushy tail was wrapped around his body and the white tip, Caidy knew was there, was tucked under his back legs. This fox had been there before. Crystal had never let Nate shoot the fox. She would make him use a "have-a-heart" trap.

They had named him Trickster and no matter how many times they had scared him away, weeks later he always showed up again. Nate let out a yell and Trickster, quick as lightning jumped up and ran under the pasture fence and disappeared into the dark night. As, her eyes followed the disappearing fox, she saw the silhouettes of the horses in the pasture, slowly walking, heads lowered as they grazed.

She shivered under her thin t-shirt and light jacket. The nights were starting to get cold, telling her the freezing Colorado winter was starting to move in.

"Good thing you saw him before he somehow got into the chicken house," Nate said to Caidy as they walked back into the warm kitchen.

"Yeah," she said as she shrugged off her black jacket and got back to work on the dishes as Nate walked into the dining room. When she had washed, dried and put away all the dinner dishes, she walked into the dining room and sat down. The ranch hands had gone to their own small cabin in the ranch yard that they lived in, and Crystal had gone upstairs to put Tyler to bed.

As Crystal came down the stairs and saw Caidy and Nate standing, she said, "Who wants to watch a movie?"

"I do!" they both said in unison and they all laughed as they collapsed on the sofa in the living room.

"I'll make the popcorn," Caidy volunteered.

"I'll pick the movie," Nate said.

"And I'll just sit here," Crystal said happily.

Caidy laughed and walked into the kitchen. She put a bag of popcorn into the microwave and poured three glasses of root beer and set them on a pink plastic tray. When the microwave beeped, she took out the popcorn and dumped it into a bowl and then set it on the tray. She carried it into the living room and set it on the coffee table. She sat down on the sofa in the spot she had claimed as hers since the first day they had bought it.

Nate put an action movie into the player and sat down. When the snacks were long gone and the movie was over, Nate helped a sleepy Caidy up the stairs to her bed.

CHAPTER 9

A WEEK LATER, Caidy was watching Stardust in her paddock. The filly had grown so much in two weeks and had also grown more independent from her mother. Now she was running around the paddock, bucking, rearing and whinnying a lot.

Caidy was sweating in the hot late August air as she mucked out a stall, sweat ran down her forehead and rolled down her cheek. She straightened up and leaned on the pitchfork. As she wiped her forehead with the back of her hand, she looked out the ranch yard through the barn door.

Pip, for once, was lying still on his back, tongue hanging out of his white mouth. The chickens were standing around their chicken yard, looking dazed in the heavy, sticky air. Caidy knew soon things would change. Soon the ground would be frozen, the bare trees would be weighed down because they would be coated with ice, snow would be falling by the foot and it would be cold enough to give unprepared persons frostbite.

Caidy personally could not wait. She loved the cold and snow and ice – so did their horses. The Colorado-bred horses loved galloping in the white snow, their hooves kicking it up into the crisp winter air.

Crystal and Caidy both took professional photographs of the horses and the Colorado snow. That is how they made some of their income. They would send them in huge frames off to Denver and they would sell at art auctions for hundreds, sometimes even thousands of dollars. As she wheeled the heavy wheelbarrow out of the stall and into the next one, she thought; Kimmy would be back in a few days. They had found they had so much in common, her grandmother had insisted she would have to stay longer.

Then the week after she came back, school would start. Then autumn would come and then winter after that. That reminded her. She and Crystal were going into town today to shop for school supplies. Caidy couldn't wait. She loved shopping for school supplies. All the new notebooks and pens and pencils and folders and everything. She was one of the weird teens that actually did not mind school. She was great at gym, English, science, history and geography, math, everything. She was going into 10th grade, her sophomore year at Bailey High School. They had a great football team, the Coyotes, who had been state champions the year before. The school in Bailey was a middle school and also a high school. There was an elementary school across town. There was just one downfall, Maddison Randall would be moving up too. She was, in Maddison and her group's opinion, the queen of Bailey High School. Caidy had a meet-the-teachers thing the coming Saturday. She loved good teachers and could not stand mean ones.

When she was done mucking out the stall, she walked out the back barn door. She dumped the wheelbarrow into the muck pile and parked the wheelbarrow and hung up the pitchfork and broom onto the barn hooks. She went up to the house, took a shower, changed clothes, took out her silver earrings and put in silver dangly teardrop-shaped earrings, put on a flick of mascara and grabbed her purse. She did not know why, but whenever she went into town, she wanted to look nice. Crystal met her out in the hall, also in nice clothes.

"You ready?" Crystal asked happily.

"Yep." Caidy answered.

When they walked downstairs into the living room, they saw Nate sitting on the sofa with Tyler on his lap, playing with toy cars and the military channel was playing on the T.V. Major Daddy-little-guy time. They strolled outside, Crystal to the garage and Caidy out toward her horse. Moonlight was standing at the fence, his head hung over it, watching Caidy approach.

"Hey, big boy," Caidy said, brushing away his forelock and rubbing the star on his forehead. His leg was un-bandaged and almost healed. She would be able to let him in the pasture the next few days since the veterinarian had come the day before and passed him as perfectly healthy, so he could be put with the other horses. Crystal pulled up in her convertible powder blue Ford Mustang. Caidy opened the front door, hopped in and they drove off.

* * *

As the silver stallion watched his herd, a hawk soared on the drafts of hot air that made it soar higher and higher and then made him disappear. The stallion lowered his head and drank deeply from the surprisingly cold stream. A big soft-shelled turtle sat on a log that had wedged itself into the black sandy shore. The turtle watched the stallion that drank from his stream. His brown head stretched out and he slowly walked to the edge of the log as he dove into the cold stream.

His webbed feet pushed him through the water with amazing speed for a turtle, and he quickly disappeared as he swam upstream. The silver stallion lifted his head as water droplets dripped from the long whiskers on his grey muzzle. He trotted through his herd of mustang mares and fillies. He now considered this herds his because he knew the stallion who had ruled before was not coming back.

* * *

At the store, Caidy took a notebook off the shelf and looked at the cover. She smiled. There was an appaloosa stallion running through pine trees in gently falling snow, his hooves kicking up clouds of snow. She had taken this picture and sold it to an office supplier. The stallion was called Silent Thunder. It was the best picture she had ever taken of a horse. She put it into the small shopping cart along with a package of red striped pencils. When they were done shopping, they walked out to the car loaded down with shopping bags.

They ate lunch at Biggie Burger and then went clothes shopping at Mustang mall.

She walked out with three more pairs of jeans, tons more shirts and headbands.

As they sat at one of the three stop lights in Bailey, Caidy looked around at her hometown. There was Mustang mall, a Biggie Burger, a small strip mall, a bank, a single apartment house and a couple of other buildings, not including the schools. If anyone wanted a big town, they would have to make the hour drive to Denver. The only thing between here and there was miles and miles of open range, towering mountains and a few small towns like Bailey sprinkled here and there.

As they drove under the sign that marked Starlight Ranch, Caidy looked at all the horses in the pasture that lined the long red dirt driveway. As they hopped out of the car and started unloading all her new stuff, Nate came out and helped them. After all the shopping bags were in her room, she went downstairs and outside to Moonlight's corral carrying the felt halter.

She had been doing a training session with Moonlight at the same time every single day for the past two weeks. Now he simply sauntered over to her and practically shoved his head into his blue felt halter. Caidy led him around his corral and dropped back to his shoulder as he kept walking at the same pace. She gently put her hands on his back. She walked twice around the corral with her hands on his back. Then, she moved up to his head and went around the corral again. He looked like he was trying to figure out what she was doing. Then she did it again and gently applied some pressure. He stopped and looked over his shoulder at her. She walked to his head again and led him around one more time.

"Good boy," She said as she fed him a bright orange carrot and petted his sleek black neck. She opened the corral gate and then led him out towards the large pasture.

She opened the pasture gate and sure enough, Dixie was standing, ready to greet her new pasture mate. She nickered welcomingly as Caidy opened the gate and led him in.

Dixie squealed in excitement and trotted over to him. After Caidy slipped off the halter, Dixie sniffed his muzzle. Moonlight whiffed back and they both trotted off to the far side of the pasture where the other horses grazed. Caidy watched the pair disappear over a rolling hill that blocked her vision to the other side of the pasture.

She hung up the blue felt halter in the tack room and took out a brand new white halter with the stallion's name engraved on a small silver plate. She had bought it at the tack shop in Bailey and it would be Moonlight's new halter. She would show it to him the next day.

She went to the house and upstairs. She peeked into Tyler's room during his nap time, expecting him to be asleep in his baby crib. Instead, she saw the cubby little baby laying on his tummy, wide awake with his little head held up high, looking around his nursery with his big blue eyes. When he saw Caidy standing in the doorway, he smiled that huge, genuine smile that all happy babies smile. Caidy walked into the room and looked down into the crib.

"Hey, little baby boy. You're supposed to be taking a nap. You already took one with daddy, didn't you?" she asked the grinning baby. He only beamed bigger, wiggled a little and made some sort of a laughing noise.

"Silly boy," Caidy laughed as she lifted him out of the crib. He held onto her as if his life depended on it as she carried him out into the hall and into her room. She set him down on his baby blanket that was blue, incredibly soft and had little fluffy white lambs on it. She set down several beanie baby horses in front of him. He instantly reached out, grabbed it and started chewing on a white one.

Caidy started cutting tags off her new clothes and hung them up in her closet. She wrote her name and address on the tag in her new black backpack. She was babysitting Tyler because her mom and dad had gone out on a "date night" and her grandparents were out of town. The sun was starting to go down when Tyler fell asleep. She laid him in the playpen in the living room. She turned on the T.V. and turned the volume down. She made herself a dinner of macaroni and cheese and picked a jar of baby food for Tyler. She tried to pick one out that would not completely gross her out; squished blueberries and pears. That wasn't too bad, she thought. Then she opened it. The smell almost made her sick. Tyler started crying from the other room. "You said it, buddy," she said to him through the door.

When the timer finally beeped, she pulled the hot macaroni off the stove with her bare hands. "Oh, wow! Man, that's hot," she said as she dropped it on the counter. She shook her hands as if that would help. She left the pan on the counter to cool off, grabbed a bib that said "I love ponies" in blue letters and a little spoon and walked into the living room.

Tyler was lying on his tummy, his head held high. Little tears were dropping from his fat little cheeks and his face was beet red as he cried.

"Oh, it's okay, little buddy," she said as she picked him up. She jiggled him on her waist until he stopped crying. She set him down in his high chair, buckled him in and clipped on his bib. She opened the jar of baby food and started feeding him. Fifteen minutes later, Tyler's mouth and Caidy's hands were stained purple, but Tyler had amazingly eaten more than was smeared on his mouth. She wiped off his mouth and her hands and took off his bib. She lifted him out of the high chair and carried him up the stairs to his nursery.

She laid him in his crib and turned on the mobile that hung above it and sang a lullaby. After a little while, he finally closed his eyes and fell asleep again. Caidy turned off the mobile, the main light and turned on the small night light and the intercom. She went downstairs and wiped off the high chair and went to get her macaroni and cheese. It was cold. She put it back into the microwave and poured herself a glass of root beer. She looked out the kitchen window and saw Moonlight's empty corral. He was in the pasture, but she wished she was able to see him. She got her macaroni and root beer. She carried it into the living room and turned on the T.V.

*   *   *

Moonlight galloped across the pasture countless of times with the other Starlight Ranch horses in the dark crisp night. Hoof beats made the ground under the horses tremble as they raced across the pasture. An owl with large glowing eyes sat in an aspen tree, watching the horses as the dark silhouette of a bat fluttered across the night sky.

Magic and Stardust were settled down in their warm stall and the ranch hands were cooking their supper in their cabin. Yo-Yo was stretched out on a warm pile of saddle blankets on a high shelf in the tack room, in his favorite spot. Pip and Fizzy were snoozing in the ranch house while Caidy lay out on the sofa and watched T.V. The ranch yard was quiet and peaceful as the long night wore on.

CHAPTER 10

CAIDY WOKE UP before dawn and went through her morning routine. After she had eaten her breakfast, she leaned on the pasture fence and watched her horse. She was on the other side of the hill so she could not see the ranch house. The summer was almost over. School would start in a week. Her time with Moonlight and Stardust would be cut at least in half, maybe more, counting homework. She opened the pasture gate and walked in with a pail full of grain. She shook it and saw the horses on the far side of the pasture. When she stirred the bucket, their heads flew up and they broke into a gallop towards her.

Dixie pulled ahead of the herd as usual, but this time, a black stallion pulled ahead with her and matched her stride. Black and sorrel legs blurred together as they raced across the pasture. Moonlight inched ahead of Dixie and then was ahead by a full stride, then two. By the time the horses reached them, Moonlight was a full six strides ahead and he shoved his muzzle into the bucket. Dixie stopped right behind Moonlight looking angry. She sulked off to another end of the pasture looking hurt. It was the first time she had lost the race, ever. When Moonlight had finished eating the grain, she slipped the blue halter onto his head and led him out to his corral

She led him around the corral a couple of times and then slipped on his new white halter over the blue felt halter. Once it was on, she slipped off the felt one. He raised his head, as if he knew how good he looked. He looked like the king he was. His perfect black head that looked like it was made out of ebony was now framed with a vivid white halter. His forelock laid over some of it, making it looking even better.

Caidy tied him up to the fence and then trimmed his mane, forelock and tail, showing the white star on his forehead. She led him back out to the pasture and let him go. Dixie had been pouting in a corner of the pasture, but when the stallion was back in the pasture, her head flew up and she trotted over to him, suddenly forgetting her embarrassment. Caidy laughed as she watched the horses galloping around the pasture. The heavy hot August air in Colorado meant bugs. Lots and lots of bugs. Deerflies and mosquitoes were plentiful, buzzing at anything and everything that was alive. As she walked along the barn, she watched the knee-high weeds that grew along the back of the red barn. The green weeds waved in the hot breeze that blew across Starlight Ranch.

Caidy stopped as she saw a black tail strung out on the clump of weeds and then disappear as the creature it was attached to slithered deeper into the weeds. She continued to watch the weeds and saw a black head poke out of the other side. A long thin black tongue flickered out and tasted the air. Caidy was standing far enough so he did not smell her. A long Coachwhip snake slithered out of the weeds. He was about five feet long and beautifully shiny. Caidy shuddered. She moved a step forward and he raced towards the pasture and disappeared. Coachwhips were harmless and ate the mice that broke into and ate the grain in the tack room, so non-poisonous snakes were great on ranches. Caidy knew it, but that did not mean she had to like them.

She jogged into the barn and then into the tack room. She was going to have to clean out the tack room because Nate had seen a couple of cockroaches in there lately. When she moved a bucket from its place in the tack room, a cockroach, just slightly smaller than the state of Minnesota, skittered out into the open of the concrete floor. She shivered and made a face as she smashed it with her boot. Two hours and five more roaches later, she was done. The tack room had been cleaned and bug stuff had been sprinkled around the edges of the room. She washed her hands in the small sink and dried them with a paper towel. She took a pair of reins off their hook and walked outside into the bright afternoon sunlight.

Caidy blinked in surprise as she saw Moonlight standing at the pasture gate, waiting for her. He knew it was lesson time. She smiled happily as she opened the gate. Moonlight backed up, giving her room. She walked in and petted his shining black head. She clipped the reins onto his white halter and led him to his corral. She led him around the corral, excitement bubbling up inside of her. Soon she would ride him - very soon.

As she led him around, he could feel her excitement that traveled through the reins to his sensitive head. He started to prance and he held his head high. He knew too. Caidy wondered how he always knew everything that was going on. She guessed it was because he was a horse with wild instincts. After their lesson, she led him back to the pasture and let him loose. He galloped off to his new herd.

* * *

The silver stallion glowed in the single second after the sun had gone down and thrown the earth into the instant when the world is in a strange light when there is neither sun nor moon in the sky. His mane floated in the evening breeze. He was the perfect picture everyone dreams a wild horse would look like with the sunset facing and the advancing night creeping up behind him. The mares grazed below him and the foals, who were quickly transforming into yearlings, grazed with them, waiting for their own stallion to return.

* * *

Moonlight and his new found herd slept peacefully in the night as stars glimmered in the sky and the almost full moon hung by an invisible string. Caidy was baking a cake for Kimmy, who would return the next day. She and Mike had been planning a surprise party since the day she left. Felicia was making the banner. After Caidy put the cake in the oven, she started to clean up the kitchen that looked like a small tornado had hit it. She was so excited she almost dropped a stack of plates. The next day, she would ride Moonlight, but after Kimmy and Mike had left.

* * *

The next day, Caidy was tidying the living room for their party for Kimmy. She and Crystal taped up the banner Felicia had made and brought over the night before. Just when she had set up the lemonade and cake, the doorbell rang and she ran to open it. Kimmy, Mike and Felicia were standing at the door.

"Man, this is awesome," Kimmy said, smiling as she walked in and saw all the decorations they had put up. After they had eaten and talked, the three teenagers stood up and got ready to go riding, leaving their mothers to talk and more than likely finish off the last of the cake. Jazzy and Durango were tied to a fence and Caidy hurried to saddle Silverado. As they trotted up the road, Kimmy breathed in a deep breath of the clean, crisp mountain air she had missed so much.

"You know, I honestly don't know how people live so long in the city. You know, with the dirty air and all the cars and everything. I'm surprised I didn't get run over by one of the trillions of buses there."

"Yeah, it's so much better here with coyotes and rattlesnakes to be bitten by and cliffs to fall off of," Mike joked.

"No, in some ways it's worse, in more way's better." Caidy said, joining the talk.

"Yeah, exactly," Kimmy said. "But I'd rather go by a rattlesnake than by a bus any day." Kimmy said seriously while making a face at Mike. Caidy and Mike laughed at her.

"Me. too." Mike agreed.

"Then I make three," Caidy added as she felt her horse's smooth gait. "Race you to that boulder over there," she said as they reached a flat stretch of ground. They all moved their horses into a canter, then a gallop. Silverado inched ahead of the other two horses. Then it happened in an instant. Silverado faltered and went down. Caidy gasped as she saw the blue sky and the red and green ground blur into each other. She jumped from the saddle and hit the ground with a thud that almost knocked her teeth loose. Her knee hit her jaw where it had almost healed from the bruise she had gotten almost three weeks ago.

She tucked herself into a ball and rolled three somersaults and landed on the hard rocky ground. Her side stung as her cell phone split open and sharp pieces of plastic dug into her thigh. She carefully pulled it out, threw it on the ground and sat up. She looked over to Silverado. He was lying down on the ground.

"Oh, God," she prayed automatically. The once wild mustang, as if he had heard her, heaved himself onto nervously shaking legs. He quickly got a hold of himself, his legs stopped shaking and he looked over his grey shoulder at Caidy as if to say, 'What was that?' His saddle had been loosened and thrown cockeyes and was hanging over his side. His knees were bloody. That made two of them. Mike and Kimmy rode up and they jumped off of their horses.

"Are you okay? What happened?" they asked in unison.

"I'm fine," Caidy gasped. She realized the breath had been knocked out of her.

"Man, you sure got beat up," Mike said, as if she did not know that. She looked down at herself. Her new jeans were ripped and her knees were dripping with blood. Her arms were all scraped up and her back was bruised and she could feel it bleeding. Her ankle was twisted and it really hurt.

"Hey, your eye's gonna be black real soon." he added. All she cared about was Silverado. She could feel sorry for herself later. She walked up to his front legs. She lifted up one. It looked fine. Then she got to the other one, she gasped along with Kimmy. She heard Mike say "Dang," behind her. A sharp rock, just smaller than her fist, was wedged in his hoof. No wonder he went down. She tried to pull it out with her fingers, but it wouldn't budge.

"Hand me a hoof pick, will you?" she asked. Mike handed her one after he went over to his saddlebags. She finally pried the sharp rock out of his hoof. He might be lame for at least a week, maybe two. Caidy let his hoof drop to the ground and she stood up.

"So much for safer than the city," Caidy joked and Kimmy smiled. She held Silverado's head and looked into his one blue eye and one brown.

"I'm sorry, buddy boy," she said as she grabbed onto his reins. She swung up onto Jazzy double after she had picked up her broken cell phone. Caidy held onto his reins as he easily kept up with Jazzy. When they reached Starlight Ranch, Caidy swung off Jazzy and put Silverado into the empty corral where she used to keep Moonlight. The poor horse was starting to limp as he slowly walked into the corral.

"I'll have Dad check you out," she told him as she took off his tack.

"I'll give you a special brushing too, as soon as I get cleaned up myself," she said as her whole body throbbed in pain.

"We can take care of brushing him and cleaning him up," Kimmy volunteered.

"Thanks, guys. See ya later," she said gratefully to her two best friends in the world.

She limped up to the house, trying to act like she was not in any pain at all, but she was. As she walked into the house, she was relieved not to have anyone home yet. She did not want to have to explain what happened, not just yet. Her chin had just healed a few days ago and now she was all beat up again. Nate and Crystal could be extremely overprotective, so she would not be able to ride Moonlight until later. She knew it.

She sunk down into her favorite chair and closed her eyes. She needed to get ice for her eye. It was probably swollen to the size of a baseball. It was just her luck to have to go to her first day of high school as a sophomore with a big fat black eye.

"Hi, hon. Wow! What happened to you?" The female voice got desperate.

"Oh, hi, Mom, I didn't know you were home," Caidy said as she quickly sat up and swallowed back a squeal that threatened to pop out if she made a move like that one more time.

"What happened?" Crystal asked as she sat on the floor and looked at her daughter with extreme concern.

"I, um, just had a little spill, that's all." Caidy said, trying to make it sound like no big deal. Crystal did not take the bait.

"Which horse?"

"Silverado," Caidy admitted quietly. "He got a rock caught in his hoof." She said as she pulled out the rock from her pocket.

"Oh, honey, let me get ice for your eye, it's the size of a baseball," she said as she hurried to the kitchen. Caidy smiled. She had guessed right. She forced herself to get up from the chair and go over to the full-length mirror that was in the entry way. She gasped as she looked at her reflection. She had never seen anyone so beat up looking in real life before. On T.V., sure, but not in real life. Her knees and her arms were torn to pieces, and her black eye was as black as Moonlight with red, blue, and purple smears in some places. She practically crawled up the stairs and sat on her bed. Crystal came up the stairs with a bag of ice and bandages. Half an hour later, Caidy was all bandaged up and was holding ice on her eye.

"Wow," she heard a voice say as she lay on the sofa watching T.V.

She turned around and saw Nate standing in the living room looking at her. "Your mom told me what happened. I talked to her," Caidy listened, not knowing where he was headed.

"We know you really want to, so we agreed that when you feel up to it, you can ride Moonlight. Just around the ranch, though." Caidy was amazed. She jumped up and hugged her dad. He smelled like horses, leather and fresh mountain air. As she backed away, Nate smiled a flashing white smile. She collapsed on the sofa again, resting up for the night. She was going to feel "up to it" if it killed her.

* * *

When Caidy carefully walked out to the barn in the dusk, she took in all the horses looking at her with heads swung over their stall doors. She dumped dry cat food into Yo-Yo's dish and she appeared out of nowhere and started eating. Caidy changed her water in the tack room sink. She lifted the reins off the hook and almost dropped them in her excitement. She had kept Fizzy and Pip inside the house so they would not make her wild stallion nervous. She walked out to the pasture. Moonlight, as if he knew what was about to happen, was standing at the fence, ready. An owl hooted in the ever darkening night and crickets started their singing.

She opened the gate and walked into the pasture. She looked over her shoulder and saw Nate, Crystal and Tyler sitting on the porch, watching her. Caidy could not see it in the dark, but she knew Nate had a satisfied smile on his deeply tanned face, she could feel it. She looked back over to the stallion she loved. Moonlight's black coat glimmered in the soft light that was made by the full moon that hung in the dark, star studded sky. He had an excited look in his brown eyes. He was ready.

She clipped the reins onto his halter. He stood still as she put her hands on his back and applied some pressure. He blew through his lips as if to say, "Come on already!"

She held the reins firmly in her hand and took a deep breath. She swung up onto the tall stallion. Her heart skipped a beat. She was riding him! She gently squeezed her legs and leaned forward. He took off at a gallop through the cold night air. She twisted her fingers with his coarse black mane. He galloped through his domestic herd and then completed his loop back the gate. She opened it, guided him through and closed it again.

Caidy looked to the porch. Her dad had moved into the glow of the porch light and was standing, leaning on a post. He smiled and nodded. She grinned and urged Moonlight forward. She raced down the dark road as they set out on their first moonlight ride.

ABOUT THE AUTHOR

HI! I'M LEXI Bassford. I was born in Wichita, Kansas in 1994. When I was 11 years old, my family moved to Trinity, Florida, where I still live and write. This is my first book – but I'm planning on writing a lot more.

Just for the record, I don't really like the kind of "About the Authors" where they just give you their name, age, and location. I want to tell you all some things about me! So, this is my letter to you!

I have a Corgi, Gracie, who I modeled Fizzy after. I have been obsessed with horses all my life. I love listening to country, Christian and a little bit of every other kind of music, going to the beach, cooking, writing, horseback riding, swimming and hanging out with all of my amazing friends. My family loves the Lord and each other.

I don't let the fact that I'm only 14 years old stop me from writing books. Hey, if you want to write and are determined enough to finish a book, why not do it? Writing is actually pretty easy. You think up something and then you put it down on paper. That's all there is to it. If you're scared of getting writer's cramp, get a computer – if you get writers cramp on that, let me know! Sometimes I lay awake at night just thinking. Then the next morning, I put it down on paper.

For my books, I weave my real life, my dreams, my experiences, etc. into one thing and make a book. For instance – one of my best friend's last name is McKinney and I do know a guy Mike (we call him Michael, though) and on a beauty pageant one year, I saw the name Caidy and thought it was pretty cool.

My dad, Robert Bassford (he's written some books, too) taught me a system that really works. You carry around index cards and a small pen in either your pocket or purse and when, say, you're standing in line at a restaurant and you have an awesome idea, you can write it down and file it later. I keep a notebook where I write all of my ideas, no matter what about. Remember to date them! Because, believe me, you probably won't be able to remember it when you get home and are sitting in front of your laptop or pad of paper. I always get hit with my best ideas when I don't expect them.

I'm home schooled and I have been for my entire life. I was a freshman in high school (when I finished this book). I love it, we learn so much without even leaving the house (even though we still do☺). Whenever I tell someone my age that, the usual response is this: "No way, that is so not fair!" and sometimes the response is: "Man, that's great, but, how do you socialize?" You know what? Home schoolers do socialize! We go to the movies, youth groups, the beach, and the mall, same as everybody else. Once a week, we go to a home school co-op. We do things you can't really do with only four people, like Spanish, art, PE and other stuff. We all socialize, have lunch together and hang out. So, yes, homeschoolers do socialize with everyone. The one thing I don't like is this: when you tell someone you're home schooled and they say, "Wow, I bet you can go to school in your PJ's, right?" NO! We totally do take school seriously. We do get grades and we do pass and (sometimes) fail tests.

I live on about an acre of land and I don't have a horse (yet), but I've wanted one for as long as I can remember. There's a palomino horse down the street named Princess and I go down to see her all the time.

If you have something you live and breathe, like horses, write about it! Everyone has something they're obsessed with. It could be the mall, the beach or trees or something. Examples: "Malls of America: The Complete Guide" or, "Why Dolphins are Awesome" and even "Save the Trees, Use Plastic!" would work, too. If you want to be heard about something, usually the best way to make people listen is to write it down.

Okay, enough of me, but when you're done with this book, I'll probably have Moonlight.com set up. There'll be quizzes, contests, those awesome little picture thingies that you print out and color, poster books and calendars and cool stuff like that and this thing where you can e-mail me with questions regarding anything and everything about horses and I'll do the best I can to answer! ☺

You can buy my books, this one and the one coming up next, Untamed, and all that I'm planning on writing after them. Thanks for reading this whole long book I wrote!

Remember, if you want to write, go for it!

~Lexi Bassford

HORSE FACTS

Horse Talk!

IF YOU'VE SPENT anytime around horses, you have probably noticed that horses communicate with the people and other horses around them. They try to tell you how they feel – if they feel sick, hurt, happy, annoyed and anything else. All you've got to do is listen!

Blow – Usually one huge exhale, like a snort.
Possible Meanings: "Hey, what was that?", "Whoa!", "So there!", "Ooh, that feels good!", "Yikes!"

Grunts, groans, sighs, and sniffs – Usually grunts and groans are like human grunts and groans, they are usually just expressions of boredom, excitement, annoyance or just to do it!

Whinny – A loud, long horse call that can be heard from up to half a mile away! Horses often whinny back and forth and sometimes, to greet their humans.
Possible Meanings: "Is that you over there?", "Hello! I'm over here!", "See me? I see you!"

Neigh – A neigh is basically the same as a whinny.

Nicker – This is the friendliest and most loving greeting a horse can give you. A nicker is a low sound made in the throat that makes a rumbling sound. As a horse

owner you might hear a nicker around feeding time. If you want a horse to love you, this is the sound you want to hear.
Possible Meanings: "Welcome back! Good to see you; I missed you.", "Hey, there, come on over here.", "Oh, I love you!", "Got anything good to eat?"

Squeal – A high-pitched cry that sounds like a scream can be heard from over a hundred yards away.
Possible Meanings: "Don't you dare!!", "Stop it!", "I'm warning you!", "Ouch, that hurts!", "I've had it!"

Horses can also communicate without using sounds, just like humans. When you shrug your shoulders, wink, roll your eyes, even give a rock-on sign, they all mean something. It's the same with horses. Sure, more than likely they won't give you a rock-on sign when you walk into the barn in the morning but they do have a secret language of their own. You'll need to observe each horse and tune into the individuality of each horses personality and actions, but here are some possible versions of non-verbal horse talk.

EARS

Flat back ears – When a horse pins back its ears, beware! If ears just go back slightly, the horse must just be irritated. The closer the ears are pressed to the skull, the angrier the horse is. That's his warning for you to get away – he's ready to bite.
Possible Translations: "I don't like that buzzing fly.", "You're making me mad!", "I'm warning you!", "Don't do that, or I'll make you wish you hadn't!"

Pricked forward, stiff ears – Ears stiffly forward usually means the horse is on alert. Something ahead has captured its attention.
Possible Translations: "What's that?", "Did you hear that?", "I want to know what that is!" Forward ears also might say, "I'm cool and I know it!"

Relaxed, loosely forward ears – When a horse is content, listening to sounds all around him, ears relaxed, tilting loosely forward.
Possible Translations: "Nope, nothing new here."

Uneven ears – When a horse swivels one ear up and one ear back, it's just paying attention to the surroundings and trying to find something to pay attention to.
Possible Translations: "Sigh; so, anything interesting going on here yet?"

Stiff, twitching ears – If a horse twitches stiff ears, flicking them fast (in combination with overall body tension) be on guard! The horse might be frightened and ready to bolt.
Possible Translations: "Yikes!", "I'm outta here!", "Head for the hills!'

Airplane ears – Ears lopped to the sides usually means the horse is bored or tired.
Possible Translations: "Nothing exiting ever happens around here.", "So, what's next already?", "Bor-ing!", "Entertain me!"

Droopy ears – When horse's ears sag and droop to the sides, it may just be sleepy, or it may be in pain.
Possible Translations: "Yawn . . . I am soooo sleepy.", "I could sure use some shuteye!", "I don't feel so good."

TAIL

Tail twitches hard and fast – An intensely angry horse will twitch its tail hard enough to hurt anyone who's not paying attention and is in striking distance. The tail flies side to side and maybe up and down as well.
Possible Translations: "I've had it, I tell you!", "Enough is enough!", "Stand back and get out of my way!"

Tail held high – A horse that holds her tail high may just be glad to be a horse!
Possible Translations: "Get a load of me!", "Hey, everybody, just look how gorgeous I am!", "I'm so amazing and darn proud of it!"

Clamped-down tail – Fear can make a horse clamp down her tail to her rump.
Possible Translations: "I don't like this – it's scary!", "What are they going to do to me?", "Can someone help me?", "Hey, crazy, what are you doing?"

Pointed tail swat – One sharp, well aimed tail swat can mean something hurts there.
Possible Translations: "Ouch! That hurts!", "I finally got that pesky fly!"

Other Signals

Pay attention to other signals given by your horse. Stamping a hoof may mean impatience or eagerness to get going. A rear hoof that is raised slightly off the ground means the horse is relaxed and laid back. When a horse is angry or scared, their muscles get tense, their back stiffens, and their eyes flash, showing extra whites of their eyes. One anxious horse may balk; standing statue-still and stiff legged. Another horse just as anxious may dance sideways or paw the ground.

A horse in pain might swing his head backwards toward the pain, toss his head, shiver, or try to rub and nibble the sore spot. Sick horses tend to lower their heads and look dull, listless and unresponsive.

As you start to communicate with your horse and try to understand all of her body language and sounds. Remember that all horses may use the same action to say totally different things. For example, one horse may plaster his ears to his head when another would tilt her ears backwards to listen to her rider. Each horse has her own language, and it's up to you to understand her. Good luck! ☺

Markings!

God made beautiful markings for horses. From an upside-down heart on the forehead to striped hooves, there are a lot of awesome markings, so lets get started!

FACIAL MARKINGS:

Star: A star is a small white marking on the forehead, often diamond shaped. (So why's it called a star, would someone tell me?)

Stripe: A narrow, white line that reaches from the top of the head to the end of the nose

Blaze: A wide white line that extends down the middle of the face, usually extending from the top of the head to the upper lip.

White face: Similar to the blaze, only wider.

Snip: A small white marking between the nostrils. (Very cute!)

White nostril: White markings around the nostril, similar to a snip.

White muzzle: A completely white muzzle

Mealy muzzle: A light brown muzzle area; often seen in the Exmoor pony.

Lip marks: White markings on and/or around the lips.

Wall eye: Usually one of the eyes has white or blue coloring instead of the normal eye color.

Sclera: The outer membrane of the eyeball is white and is often seen in Appaloosas.

BODY MARKINGS:

Black points: Black socks or stockings, black mane and tail, black muzzle and black tips on the ears, often seen on bay horses.

Flaxen mane and tail: The mane and tail are of light cream color – often seen on chestnut horses.

Dorsal or eel stripe: A black or dark brown stripe that extends from the withers along the back bone and down into the tail – often seen on dun horses. Wither stripes sometimes accompany dorsal stripes – these are lines extending across the withers on either side.

Dapples: Dark circles or rings that appear over lighter areas of the body. Most commonly seen in grays, they can occur in any coat coloring, especially bay and are usually more visible in the spring or autumn, when the horse is changing his coat.

Whorls: Sometimes called 'cowlicks,' these are terns formed by irregular hair growth. They may be seen along the crest and underside of the neck, although they can appear anywhere on the body and are used for identification, too.

LEG MARKINGS

White sock: Front or hind limbs are white from the coronet band upward to any point below the knee or hock

White stocking: Front or hind limbs are white from the coronet band upward to above the knee or hock.

White coronet: The area of the coronet band is white.

Ermine marks: Black or brown dots that appear on or around the coronet or pastern on a white sock.

Zebra marks: Rings of dark hair appearing around the lower leg which are associated with primitive or feral breeds.

HOOF MARKINGS

Blue hoof: The hooves are a slate blue-black color. Blue hooves are considered denser and stronger than white hooves, although there is no scientific proof.

White hoof: The hoof has a white horn. This is often seen where there is a white marking on the legs.

Striped hoof: The hooves have vertical black and white striped running up and down the hooves this is often associated with the Appaloosa and other spotted horses.

Well, I hope that this has taught you more about horses and you will get closer to your horse or the horses at your local riding stable.
    Remember, always stay safe and aware when around horses and always, always have fun!!

~Lexi Bassford

CPSIA information can be obtained
at www.ICGtesting.com
Printed in the USA
LVOW11s1359281117
557877LV00003B/141/P